THE CONTEMPORARY
ART OF THE NOVELLA

THE CONTEMPORARY ART OF THE NOVELLA

# THE
# PATHSEEKER

# THE
# PATHSEEKER

TRANSLATED, WITH AN AFTERWORD, BY TIM WILKINSON

**MELVILLE**HOUSE
BROOKLYN, NEW YORK

ORIGINALLY PUBLISHED UNDER THE TITLE *A NYOMKERESŐ*.
PUBLISHED BY PERMISSION OF ROWOHLT VERLAG GMBH,
REINBEK BEI HAMBURG.

DESIGN: BLAIR AND HAYES, BASED ON A SERIES DESIGN BY DAVID
KONOPKA

MELVILLE HOUSE PUBLISHING
145 PLYMOUTH STREET
BROOKLYN, NY 11201

WWW.MHPBOOKS.COM

FIRST MELVILLE HOUSE PRINTING: APRIL 2008

LIBRARY OF CONGRESS CATALOGING-IN-PUBLICATION DATA
KERTÉSZ, IMRE, 1929-
  [NYOMKERESO. ENGLISH]
  THE PATHSEEKER / IMRE KERTESZ ; TRANSLATED BY TIM
WILKINSON.
      P. CM.
  ISBN 978-1-933633-53-4
  I. WILKINSON, TIM. II. TITLE.
  PH3281.K3815N913 2008
  894'.511334--DC22

                              2008007028

THE PATHSEEKER

## VISITING

The host—a man with a complicated family name, Hermann by Christian name—was chattering ingenuously; it seems he really did still take his guest to be only a simple colleague, and the latter, puffing on his pipe (a tiresome implement but, it had to be admitted, one that on occasion was quite indispensable) quietly studied his face. He did not see it as anything special: it was the face of a middle-aged man that radiated an untroubled self-confidence, oval in shape, ordinary nose and mouth, brown hair, blue eyes. As yet it was impossible to tell for sure if behind the show of chattering was concealed the usual trickery or merely infantile naïveté; he inclined toward the latter assumption, though in point of fact—he reflected—the difference between the two was negligible. He cast another glance at him: did he really seriously believe he had finally managed to cut the strings? Well, it made no difference; he would soon have to learn that the strings never could be cut and that, like all witnesses, sooner or later he, too, would have to confess.

He donated another minute to him, a single minute of unclouded freedom from care. He paid attention to his chatter; he was chattering about his occupation, or, to be more precise, the difficulties of his occupation, with the confidence, if maybe not of an accomplice, then of a colleague, pretending to be immensely concerned on their account—that is to say, pretending to have not a care in the world. Crafty, the guest granted, very crafty; it was not going to be easy to break him, that was for sure. He swept his eyes over the scene: the moment seemed opportune, with the two of them sitting in spruce-green leather armchairs in one corner of the room, behind a coffee table, while in another corner the wives were trying out shoes on each other's feet, totally absorbed in this female whimsy. Yes, it was time to set to work.

He took the pipe from his mouth and cut him short with calm, premeditated hostility. He then informed him in a single terse sentence who he was and the object of his mission and the investigation that he was to pursue. Hermann turned slightly pale. He soon pulled himself together, though, as was only to be expected: to some extent the unexpected announcement had caught him off-guard, for up till now all the signs suggested that the guest—the colleague—had come to the small town merely on account of the specialist conference that had just ended, as a result of which, offhand, he could not think what to say at this late hour . . .

"And after so many years," the guest interjected.

"Just so! I can't deny that either," Hermann responded. "But one thing intrigues me before we go any further: Am I under any obligation at all to answer your questions?"

"No," came the quick answer. "Your own laws are the only ones applicable to you. You should definitely be cognizant of that, and it's inexcusable of me not to have said so at the start."

Hermann thanked him, he had merely been curious, and now, he declared with a smile, he was ready to give evidence, voluntarily and freely, as his guest could see. True, the guest agreed, though maybe with less appreciation than Hermann, for all his magnanimity, had no doubt been expecting. The guest was evidently of the opinion—surprising self-assurance—that Hermann would give evidence in any event. But that was precisely what was baffling. He asked nothing, just carried on calmly sitting there, sucking his pipe, looking almost bored.

Hermann broke the silence a minute later. What, in point of fact, he inquired, would be of interest to his guest? Would he like, perhaps, he pumped further, seeing that the guest was putting off giving an answer, as if he were still weighing something up, to quiz him, Hermann, about some personal questions? Or maybe, he continued with a ready, conciliatory little smile in anticipation of understanding, to ascertain what he, Hermann, knew, and how much?

"Well, certainly," he responded. "Of course, I'd be glad to listen, insofar as you are indeed in the mood to talk about it."

"Why not?" Hermann shrugged. After all, he had nothing to hide. Though it therefore followed, he added, that he did not have much to say either. There was no denying that he had heard about the case. He also knew that it had happened around there. It was painful, still painful, even to talk about it. He personally had not been able to devote much attention to it at the time. He did not wish to burden his guest with explanations, but at any rate he had good reason, at the time, for instance, to say no more; he had still been more or less a child, which was no excuse, of course, merely a circumstance, but it might go some way to explaining it. Even so, naturally, one thing and another had come to his attention. He heard that something had happened, despite the numerous impediments—indeed, it might be true to say that precisely through their conspicuous presence—it had been impossible for a person not to become aware of certain things, albeit involuntarily. Anyone who said any different was lying. However, the details and the scale, which is to say the case itself, had actually only started to assume their true shape later on.

At this point, Hermann relapsed into silence for a minute; perhaps to give himself a fixed point to rest on at last, he interlaced his constantly mobile hands, which had been providing a running commentary to accompany everything he said, around a knee that he had pulled up as he sat there, and a quiet popping of his knuckles was clearly audible before he commenced speaking again.

He could have done what others had done and just ignored the matter. Who could reproach him for that? But, he carried on, something had given him no respite; something had driven him, troubled him—curiosity, but no, that wasn't the right word for it, yet this wasn't the place for being modest, so was it all right for him to speak instead about duty, the agonizing duty of knowledge? He had set about feverish research: he had sought facts, indisputable facts above all, in order to see his way clearly in the matter. He had collected files, acquired evidence, accumulated an entire archive—there were things to show to the guest. All that was missing now was to work up this heap of objective evidence; it was just . . . Hermann sighed deeply, leaned back in his seat without letting go of his knee, and closed his eyes for a minute as if they were being bothered by the strong lamplight. "It's just that even with the hypothesizing," he continued, "we are going a long way, rather too far in fact. One had certain thoughts: one can't help it. And although those thoughts don't stem from yourself. . . it's just . . . how to put it? You understand? In other words . . . there's something intimidating about this. Something stirs inside . . . some inner protest . . . a feeling that I find hard to put a name to offhand . . . I'm afraid I am not making myself clear enough . . ."

He fell silent again, casting an unsure glance at the guest, and although the latter was careful that no comment of his should exercise any influence, Hermann seemed to have read encouragement from his expression, because he continued:

"Perhaps it's the fact," he said, "that it's possible. Yes, the fact that we surmise the impossible, and all of a sudden we gain proof that . . . that it's possible. I think," working himself into a fever, "that I've managed to capture that certain feeling." He leaned forward, very close to the guest, his eyes burning with a strange light, his voice switching to a whisper. "The possibility, you catch my drift? Nothing else, the mere possibility. And that what happens just once, to just one person, has now transcended the frontiers of the possible, is now a law of reality . . ." He broke off, staring ahead, almost crushed, before again lifting his still slightly troubled eyes to the guest. "I don't know if you understand what I'm getting at . . ."

"Of course I understand," the guest nodded. "Thought-provoking and, moreover, probably true, because on what else would our constant anguish feed if we did not all feel we had a small part in universal evil?"

"Yes, yes! I see you understand me completely!" Hermann exclaimed, stretching out his hands in sudden delight toward the guest, then, perhaps failing to find the actual target of this exuberant motion, withdrew them: "I'm glad we met, glad you're here! Indeed, you ought to have come sooner, I'd say!"

"That was impossible," the guest apologized.

"There was a lot we needed to talk about, a lot! There was a time when I was very much expecting . . . expecting your arrival virtually any day!"

"I'm sorry, but only now did its turn come round," the guest defended himself.

"Pity. It doesn't matter now, but it's a pity." Hermann slowly overcame his emotions, his words again falling into intelligible order, like the stones of a building. Well, yes: such a great burden, he said, and so little opportunity for any determined, resolute deed. He had fretted, nagged more and more by the question of what more could he do, over and above what a person does anyway from day to day, but to tell the truth he had not had much success. And then he had been obliged to turn his attention to life's other demands: he had worked his way up from a lowly position, he had studied, made a living and eventually started a family—all of which had cost no small amount of his energy, to be sure, to get him to where he was today. He did not want his guest to misunderstand and to interpret his words as meaning that, as far as he was concerned, he had therefore set the matter aside for good; no, he hadn't, and it went without saying that he was eager to undertake any service, without reservation, that might be incumbent on him as a result of the consequences of the case, but—and he wanted to stress this—voluntarily and independently, of course, in the same way that he was submitting himself to this deposition. He flashed a wryly meditative grin:

"How did you put it just now? Due to the part of universal evil that falls to our lot? Yes, you may be right, maybe for that reason, or in other words," Hermann carried on, led by essentially a broadly—some people, his wife for instance, would say too broadly—interpreted sense of duty, because in fact nothing tied him directly to the case, but that was already clear; there was no need to go over that again. Now that, though it might not be a lot, was just about all that he was able to say for his part, he concluded.

"Thank you," said the guest, "that was most interesting. In truth, your personal case is not part of the investigation's brief, and you no doubt recall that I merely went along with this, I didn't ask you to submit your defense; but then you no doubt felt it necessary, and why should I deny you that small favor. All the same, I thank you; it was most interesting," he reiterated.

Hermann looked at him in astonishment.

"My defense . . . ?" He knitted his brow. "I hope you don't doubt my word?" he went on to ask. "Should you wish to see my documents . . ."

"My authority doesn't cover that," he was interrupted. "The information that I have gathered about you, by the way, tallies completely with what you said. You are above suspicion, Hermann."

Well, he was very glad to hear that, said Hermann, immediately adding that it was not for personal reasons, needless to say, for there could never have been any suspicion in that regard, but in the wider sense that they had been talking about just before; that is to say, he was glad that he had not fallen prey to some wild whisper, certain prejudices, the usual tendency to generalize by which those kinds of conjectures were in the habit of being extended from individuals to families, from families to districts, and then to entire peoples, which would have grieved him tremendously.

"I understand," the guest remarked. "I too have some experience in that respect. That sort of thing is always unpleasant."

Indeed, Hermann agreed, and a person can get entangled in seemingly interminable procedures, assuming we are not indifferent in some respects, and place weight on an unblemished reputation.

"But then," he continued, "it's probably unnecessary for me to remind a colleague of the chronic shortage of time that is inseparable from our line of work. As it happens, it's rough on me right now because I'm on the brink of promotion and having to take over a new department."

The guest briefly interjected to wish him good luck.

"Thank you," Hermann acknowledged, bowing as he sat and then leaning back comfortably in the armchair, very much at home as he stretched his slippered feet out before him. "Irrespective of that, I shall naturally be at your disposal in all respects and all manner of means, as far as it lies within my power."

The guest hastened to assure him that he in no way wished to make undue demands on either his time or his patience; it was only a matter of a few pieces of information that he would like to ask his host on the matter of the site inspection, as the first visit to the scene would have to take place the next day. Then he would need to make a second inspection, to another, more distant site, but leave that for now, we should speak about the first, which he needed to make here, in the neighborhood. What he would like to know was whether everything was still on hand, intact and untouched?

"To be sure," replied Hermann, adding: "We saw to that."

Quite right, said the guest, that's very important, if not the *most* important circumstance, since obliterating the traces is one of the enemy's favorite and most dangerous weapons, for that sort of thing could endanger the success of even the most conscientious investigation—but then, that was just what the enemy was counting on, of course.

Hermann stared pensively ahead of him as if he were mulling over what the guest had said.

"But," he then asked in amazement, "what enemy are you in fact referring to? I can assure you that in our area, that is insofar as one can speak about any substantial enemy at all . . . " The guest burst out laughing at this point. "Well all right, let's suppose . . . even then he would not have the audacity to take a risk with something like obliterating the traces, and I can vouch that providing time hasn't . . ."

"Time is a dangerous enemy," the guest cut him short.

Hermann became animated. He didn't quite see it that way, he began, with a smile that reflected an objective yet firmly contrary opinion befitting questions of principle. But the guest silenced him with a single hand gesture: right now, he declared, he did not deem it appropriate to debate the issue with Hermann. An indignant expression appeared on Hermann's face: it was evident that they had touched on one of his favorite notions, and he would gladly have expounded the views that he had formed on this subject, perhaps through laborious work; but probably what may have been even less to his taste was the manner in which he had simply been made to put a lid on it, and in his own home. For several seconds it seemed as if he were deliberating whether to remind his guest of the basic rules of good manners, but in the end, not knowing why, he did not do so. Could it have been connected with the same train of thought that led him to again put his feet below himself and slip forward in the armchair, thereby relinquishing his previous ease for a tenser posture?—that likewise did not come to light. The hearing continued. The guest was interested in precisely where the scene was located. A hesitation from the person under questioning:

"But you must know that," he said eventually in a voice that was somewhat strained but simultaneously striving to be tactful.

"Naturally," came the answer, "I shall most certainly know once I'm there. It's just the route from here to there that I'm not clear about, which I think is understandable since, after all, I'm a stranger around here. Is it, perhaps, so very complicated?"

Quite the contrary, Hermann hastened to assure him, it was very easy. One needed, before anything else, to get to the neighboring town, close by here, on the same fertile plain. And here he smiled fondly and parenthetically remarked that he hoped the tour of inspection was not going to take up so much of the guest's time that he would not have a look at the sights of said town, having a bearing as they did on our entire continent's culture. From there, he carried on in a palpably drier tone and with the hesitant features that had been seen earlier, from there it was not far to the goal: four or five miles, at the most six—something like that, he did not know exactly.

"Understandable," the guest nodded, "since on the way there you obviously had other things on your mind than to count the miles."

A minute of silence arose—almost an awkward silence, one might say. As far as that went, and to be quite frank, Hermann eventually said, he had not actually been there as yet. Was that right, the guest rejoined; then of course he begged Hermann's pardon for the thoughtless interjection. Not a bit of it, Hermann protested; he felt it was more him who perhaps, to some extent, ought to be asking for pardon. But then, if that really was the way he felt, said the guest, then Hermann could certainly not be accused of being inconsistent; at most a touch forgetful. Indeed, said Hermann, he had to admit that it looked that way, yet all the same the truth was different, and he had planned to make a visit more than once, but each and every time he had had to put it off, whether for family matters or for business commitments; in other words, reasons beyond his control. He hoped, he added, that his colleague understood that when one carried the twin burdens of a family and a responsible post, people like themselves were not always absolute masters of their own time. Indeed, said the guest, he understood that only too well; we were all the same in continually putting off genuine responsibilities for lesser ones, often for the whole of our life, and we would then become flustered if we were to ask ourselves what we had actually achieved.

"It's an inexhaustible topic," he continued, "but I fear that I have already abused your hospitality. In any event, I thank you for the valuable particulars. It was interesting, most interesting," he added as he got to his feet. Hermann too jumped up from his place, seemingly excited:

"Just a moment!" he said. "You surely can't want to go! Hang on . . . what, for heaven's sake, are you looking for?"

"My umbrella," said the guest, who meanwhile really had started walking around the room, even peeking behind the furniture, because, as far as he recalled, somewhere there he had put the object down (they had set off from their hotel in muggy weather, under a heavy, overcast sky). "You didn't happen to see it anywhere?"

"No," said Hermann with evident exasperation, striving to keep close on his heels, once almost bumping into him as the guest unexpectedly came to a standstill and swung around the other way. It was fortunate that the wives were not witnesses to this ridiculous hunt, for in the meantime, having finished with the shoes, they had gone into the other room, and from the cooing sounds filtering in from there it could be surmised that, right then, they were in the middle of coddling Hermann and his wife's little son, who had most likely been startled out of his sleep by this, because at that very moment he was crying his heart out: he had obviously misunderstood the situation. "But we still haven't spoken about anything," Hermann remonstrated. "How are you going to get there, for instance?"

"By train and bus," said the guest, still vainly looking all around. "I've been told the connections are good, and both services are fast and comfortable."

True, perfectly true, Hermann assured him. So he could see, the guest was, after all, better informed about the local transport than he had let on; all he feared was that in the sweltering heat the tortuous journey would place too great a strain on him.

The guest broke into a laugh, briefly and somberly, in the disconcerting manner he had, but at least he finally turned to face Hermann, assuring him that he had traveled there before in a much more circuitous manner. But surely he wasn't suggesting, Hermann inquired, that he had already made the trip once? Indeed, he was, precisely that, though that was quite beside the point, the guest said, visibly a little nettled. Not beside the point at all, Hermann protested, for he was only now seeing that hitherto they had been endeavoring to clarify in the abstract, at the level of principles, so to say, a thing in which his guest, evidently, was personally interested. But that had no bearing on the principles, the guest hastened to point out. Of course not, Hermann acknowledged, but now taking all that into account, he saw as even more justified the question that he had posed earlier to his guest, as to whether he was not afraid the trip might place too great a strain on him. Not at all, the guest replied; if there was anything he was afraid of it was, at most, that even fear was not a remarkable enough feeling, and in respect to the success of the next day's task it would be downright advantageous to seek, not reliefs, but circumstances that were as arduous as possible, to the point of privation, or in any event that's what he would do, if he did not have also to have some consideration for his wife.

"For that very reason! For that very reason!" Hermann seized the word. "But one can't discuss things like this . . . would you finally please be seated again?"

He hurriedly directed the guest to the armchair, and they sat down. Hermann started to thumb through a leather-bound notebook.

"Let's just see. . .so, tomorrow. Hmm. Tomorrow I really should be at a managerial review . . ." he began, at which the guest, so it seemed, again made to rise; Hermann was obliged to proceed more speedily, hurriedly one might say: "Still, if I were to phone in good and early in the morning . . . I'm on pretty good terms with my boss . . . in short, I'd be happy to run you over there by car, if you wish."

The guest, now leaning back comfortably in the armchair, indeed crossing his legs, smiled.

"That's slick, Hermann, really slick." He nodded. "'If you wish' . . . Hmm, I could say, as you did just then. Well, Hermann, a straight question deserves a straight answer: No, I don't wish."

"Am I to take it you are turning down my offer?" Hermann asked.

"I didn't say that," the guest answered. "It may be that I'll agree to your escorting me; it may be that I'll go along with your taking me, since your offer has been hanging in the air here for minutes on end. By your leave, I could almost sense it maturing inside you while you were being so kind as to search for my umbrella with me. Yes, this was exactly where the logic of our talk was heading, what it was leading up to, and I can't deny that I, too, am a bit to blame. Now, as far as wishes go: for my own part, I can assure you, there can be no question, and I have to assume it is even less the case for you, at least bearing in mind the opportunities missed so far—and no, there's no need for any apologies as I'm not reproaching you with anything. The only reason I have for mentioning all this is so that we may create order . . . clear a path, if I may put it this way, through the tangle of desires, lest our affairs become muddled up with each other; you are not the only one, for I too insist on my own independence."

Hermann looked puzzled.

"So," he asked, "what have you decided in the end?"

The guest shook his head.

"You're getting trapped in strange contradictions, Hermann. You start with independence, but then you are prepared to subject yourself to my will, and now, before you know it, to my decision. What, in point of fact, do you want? A command? Or maybe absolution. . . ? Come now, Hermann, what's the point of this hide-and-seek, this unworthy quibbling, between two adults! As if you didn't know that you'll have to come anyway—or could it be that you didn't know?"

Hermann bowed his head; there was a brief stillness.

"Yes, I did know," he answered after that, and in the glazed glint of his eyes as he again raised them the guest now saw, for the first time, a new, strange, still slightly timid but undisguisedly hostile expression. And as if, far from that bothering him, he were enjoying it, he laughed at Hermann, but differently from before, appreciatively, almost sympathetically.

"I can't be accused of anything," he said. "A sense of duty in the wider sense is a trap that we set before ourselves; at most I have given it a helping hand."

"That's vindictive of you," Hermann muttered. "I've given no cause for that."

The guest apologized: in his assignment, he said, being vindictive was, so to say, his duty, and naturally the only goal had been to dispel any misunderstanding, not to upset his host.

"Oh, all right, then!" he went on. "I'll do you that small favor: you can take me. No, don't thank me, or did you want to say something else? Nothing? That too is fine. It is perhaps unnecessary for me to warn you that we probably have a hard day in front of us tomorrow. In the course of the investigation I shall have to show you one thing and another, that is unavoidable, and the smell . . . well, there's a dreadful stench over there; hopefully we are not going to get wind of that. In any event, my advice is that you don't eat breakfast."

They agreed that Hermann would bring his car to the front of the hotel at nine o'clock the next morning. Had he understood correctly, Hermann asked, that his good wife would also be going along? Yes, the guest replied curtly, and Hermann's sagging countenance, on which creases of tiredness had suddenly stood out and which seemed truly to dissolve in the closed stuffiness of the chandelier-lit room—in response to a glimmer of hope, as it were—seemed to show a fleeting shadow of relief: that was embarrassing. Still, they could not speak any more, as the ladies had returned. Hermann's spouse, a sturdy blonde, beads of perspiration glistening on her soft white bosom, had brought the infant with her, in her arms, most likely to soothe the despair with which he had emitted such heart-wrenching sounds shortly before, and maybe also out of that obscure goal, as some wives are wont, not to allow the abiding image of mother and child to pass out of mind, thereby reminding menfolk by this embodiment of their motherly responsibility. The infant himself seemed less solemn, more bad-tempered and distracted; indeed, he was soon put back to bed. The guests took their leave (the umbrella finally turned up in the hallway), and they declined Hermann's kind offer to drive them back, saying that they wanted the walk.

Outside, there had been a change in the sky: they were greeted by a glimmering, clear summer evening; tomorrow's weather was set to be fair. On the short way to the hotel he informed his wife of the planned excursion, letting fall a few words about the town, which had once been a princely seat with many sights, and which it would not be becoming to omit from the itinerary, he gave her to understand. His wife—as he could feel from her arm, which he had linked in his own—trembled slightly; her eyes—at other times a familiar mirror—were filled with anxious questioning:

"That's not why you want to go there," she said.

"No," her husband replied. "I also have a bit of business to do in the neighborhood."

"The conference, the holiday, the whole trip—that's all been just a pretext for you to get there."

"It could be," her husband admitted. "I have to finish my work sometime," he added, his voice perhaps sounding more impatient than he had intended.

"You're talking about work, but it's something else," his wife said.

"Come on," protested the husband. "What are you suggesting?"

"I don't know. I'm scared," his wife responded, and the man hastened to reassure her that there was no reason to be alarmed: the enterprise was not dangerous, it would take only a short time, and it was not going to interfere with the excursion. His wife did not respond. What and how much did she suspect, the husband wondered.

"When are we setting off for the seaside?" the wife asked later on.

"In three days," he answered. Yes, the wife was a stubborn and very dangerous opponent: she had a lot of power and was obviously going to make use of it in order to assuage whatever was rankling her, and thus had to be endured. In that respect, Hermann, a wily customer, had unquestionably sneaked a look at his cards. He was not afraid of a fight, but that he would be obliged to resist his wife, and the fact that both of them would necessarily have to resort to trickery, while it could have no bearing on his determination, nevertheless filled him with an unnameable sorrow. They could hear music muffled by curtains and glimpsed an illuminated entrance: they had arrived at their hotel.

## TURNING POINT. FIRST TRACES.
## DIALOGUE IN THE SQUARE

The next day, the commissioner and his wife were still seated at their bountiful breakfast in the hotel dining room when a white-jacketed waiter glided nimbly over to their table to announce that the gentleman was being asked to take a telephone call.

"A moment," he said to his wife, setting knife and fork down on his plate. He crossed the room, since the telephone was in the vestibule, and stepped straight into the glass-fronted booth toward which the receptionist directed him with a broad sweep of the arm.

He lifted the receiver. "Hello, Hermann?"

"Yes," came the surprised voice from the far end of the line. "How did you know . . . ?"

"What?"

"That it was me."

"I was expecting your call," the commissioner said. "As a matter of fact, you ought to have called before now."

"Yes, but what made you think," Hermann's voice marveled, "I was going to call in the first place? That wasn't what we agreed..."

"That's as may be, but something has cropped up," the commissioner said, "if I'm not mistaken?"

"Well, yes," sounded the remote voice. "The boy..."

"The boy!"

"Yes. The boy...has been taken sick."

The commissioner grimaced. The most banal, the most obvious; one was almost of a mind to blush, he reflected.

"A pity," he spoke into the receiver. "If you had let us know just ten minutes earlier," he added, "we would have had some hope of being able to catch the morning train."

"I won't hear a word about trains," Hermann remonstrated. In truth, the only reason he was phoning was to ask if, under the circumstances, they minded starting half an hour later.

"What do you mean?" the commissioner was bewildered. "You're coming anyway?"

"Of course," Hermann answered. "That is to say... I'll explain everything later." They agreed on a time, and the surprise had not yet vanished from the commissioner's face when he sat back down at the table.

Half an hour later, the man and his wife stepped through the hotel's plate-glass swing door into the open air. The brilliant sunshine of a cloudless summer sky gleamed harshly all round—appropriate weather, highly appropriate: he hoped the oppressive heat that could be expected for noon would not be detrimental to the success of the inspection, though up there on the hill—if, that is, certain long-past regularities were still valid—one could always count on a refreshing breeze. And as if he could already feel the touch of cool air on his skin—or was it merely the thought of it, impatience, that caused it?—a light shiver went through him.

"Are you cold?" His wife looked at him.

"Me, cold?" he said with a chuckle of amazement. "In this heat?" But the question had been a reminder: he needed to take better care; his every movement was being watched.

A car windscreen glinted: it was Hermann. They brusquely greeted each other, and Hermann opened the car door for them. Clearly to make room for them, he then reached back to push a white bundle on the back seat farther over—at first glance one might have mistaken it for an innocuous package had it not been uttering sounds, plaintive and at once demanding sounds that, even in their inarticulacy, vouched for a testy rancor.

"What's that?" the commissioner started back.

"The child," Hermann replied.

The commissioner did not inquire further but climbed into the front seat, beside Hermann, while his wife took a place behind, next to the boy, at which Hermann set off and immediately shifted up into top gear, like someone in a hurry. This morning, the right-hand profile of his face that he allowed to be seen while he was keeping a constant eye on the road and continuously manipulating the steering wheel and gearshift—that too, it had to be admitted, was sometimes worth as much as a pipe—was pallid and drawn, and at the same time unfathomable, almost metallically hard. After taking several bends recklessly, they were racing along the highway, and Hermann started to speak.

"It came on suddenly," he related, the way it usually was with toddlers, no sooner than the guests had set off back the previous evening. One minute earlier there had been no sign of any problem; everything had seemed as calm and tranquil as normal. He and his wife had been tidying up; there had been time for a last drop of drink, a few tender words. It was their custom, before going to bed, to look in on the child, to lean over the cot so as to have that sight in mind when turning in to bed, and so it had been this time too. They had quietly delighted in the slumbering tot, surrendering themselves without any cares to the happy image. But something had seemed not quite right: the child had stirred, and they had asked each other why he was hiding his face so shyly. They had supposed it was the electric light and so had gone to switch that off, but the boy, all of a sudden, had opened his eyes and sounds of distress had welled up from his little throat. They had bent down toward him and tried to pacify him with cooing words, kisses, soothing caresses, but hands and lips had recoiled in horror because they could feel the tiny body was burning all over. They had run to fetch

a thermometer: thirty-nine Centigrade. They had tele-
phoned for the doctor right away, yes, the "doka-ka"
(Hermann here interjected a quick smile as he expati-
ated that for some reason the word "doctor" had entered the child's vocabulary in this odd phonetic form),
and the doctor had diagnosed an infection, an acute
but hopefully uncomplicated infection.

He fell quiet and, since the road in front happened
at that moment to be empty, cast an anxious look back
over his shoulder. He had no need to, however, for
the infant's interest seemed to have turned gradually
to the strange creature seated beside him; the crying
abated, first to snuffling, then to open-mouthed silence
before finally switching to a quickening, evermore-vol-
uble gurgling, and he began to play with the crimson-
lacquered nails, the shiny medallion dangling on the
necklace, and the enticing buttons on the clothes of
the lady bending over him.

"Well, I never!" the commissioner smiled. "The
wee rascal! Deceiving his parents with that fever last
night!"

"No, no!" Hermann protested. "This is just a tem-
porary relief, the effect of an antipyretic injection. A
full recovery's going to take long days of loving care.
For that reason, the kiddie is now on his way to the
countryside, to his granny's place, to be out in the garden, in the fresh air."

"I hope we're not forcing you to make a detour,"
the commissioner worried.

No problem, Hermann assured him; even if he
would not go so far as to say the town they had to reach

was necessarily en route, he was happy to go the long way round for their sake. They would then easily be able to reach their more immediate goal by the bus service that had been mentioned yesterday, whereas he would hurry on to have the child safely in bed as speedily as possible.

"What a lot of trouble we are putting you to!" The commissioner was apologetic. "As if you didn't have enough on your plate without us!" In his defense, he went on, it was of no service, but he could only remind Hermann that he had offered, insisted on, indeed all but forced the lift on them yesterday evening.

Hermann shrugged, raised his hands in a gesture of helplessness, then quickly replaced them on the steering wheel.

"The intention," he said, "was good. I couldn't help it if things took a different course—you can see that yourself."

"Of course," the commissioner acknowledged. "As ever, your alibi is perfect, Hermann."

A stillness ensued. Hermann's round face, the hair fluttering in the cross-draft on both sides like a winged shield, paid stony attention to the road. He accelerated in order to overtake a tractor that was pottering along in front of them, then, due to the flagrant inconsiderateness of a goods truck speeding the other way, suddenly slammed on the brakes, downshifted, swerved, and then, having straightened the car out again, with narrowed eyes and, so quietly it was as if he had not yet made up his mind whether he actually wanted them to hear or not, he muttered:

"You're not human. No, not human."

The car was now sweeping along smoothly, unimpeded, making the wind whistle. The commissioner seemed to be pondering.

"In a certain respect you are undoubtedly right, Hermann," he acknowledged.

Now it was Hermann who remained mute. His face, though, was twitching; tiny, irregular, barely visible tremors nagged at the stoniness; presumably a shadow play of some inner struggle.

"Excuse me," he finally started haltingly. "I'm nervous. I'm afraid that just before . . . anyway, no offense intended."

The commissioner jerked up his head: What was that? Was one to imagine that he wished to apologize? He racked his brains to find some sharp retort, a cutting correction, but he choked back the words that had just come to mind. He had already achieved what he wanted, after all—but then what did he want? To exact revenge? Or to gain a comrade-in-arms? Right then, as they were coming ever closer to the goal, it suddenly seemed so unimportant. They slipped wordlessly onward. Lively noises were to be heard only from the rear seat; the child, after an initial euphoric flurry, had now evidently focused his effort on a single definite target as he endeavored, with stubbornly renewed lunges, to snatch hold of the lady's eyes (maybe he was attracted by brightly shining things, the sparkle of which was enhanced even more by the brush strokes of black eyeliner around them) so as to be able to clutch them and play with them, which gave rise to many a jolly episode between the two of them—after all, women and children always come to an understanding.

He lit a cigarette, a special brand with a pungent aroma (the pipe had outgrown its timeliness, and anyway he had not brought it with him) and, leaning back comfortably in the seat, devoted his attention to the road. Would they proceed along the ancient highway, bordered by the famous avenue of plum trees that had borne fruit not only on these trees but in literature as well? Even if that were so, it was not relevant here. The poet, so often damned and anathematized, who had picked fresh, juicy plums from these trees, as he remarked in his essay about the Romantic school, had been dead for more than a century now, and therefore this avenue was that much more ancient, having stood unscathed ever since. The landscape behind it was cleverly organized, with gentle seedbeds and yellowing strips of grain deceiving the beholder with misleading images of peacefulness. Here, in the shaded courtyard of an evocative hostelry, two peasant types in high boots and ink-blue aprons were drinking something that, judging from the tankards, one could presume to be beer; then look there, all of a sudden, a wood of wide-spreading, mossy-boled trees. The ground was still covered with last year's leaf mold, a damply rotting humus, quivering shafts of light in the depths, fairytale shadows, fairy trails, and strange forms flitting inside, where the early-morning sunbeams had not yet quite been able to break through the mists. The traffic was moderate; they often had to avoid cycling farmworkers, most of them women with their usually tow-colored hair worn braided in taut rings pinned to the nape of the neck, and carefully holding down their skirts as the car passed by them. Yes, nothing remarkable: a highway that, even from an old-fashioned and, by the way, intellectual point of view, was undoubtedly esteemed, but which nevertheless served a practical function, first and foremost, was here living its innocent, mundane life at every hand—perfect, it had to be granted; flawlessly perfect.

A signpost sprang up ahead on the verge of the highway. Hermann slowed, a faint wariness the only reminder on his brightening face of the previous contretemps.

"The town," he said, and this time it would have been futile to get to the bottom of what the smile was seeking to persuade one of.

But was that really what it was, the town? They came to houses, clusters of houses, later on regular streets. The commissioner's gaze swept searchingly over everything that came before it on the road surface, the pavements, the houses, the people. Yes, the same orderliness, the same perfection, the same impenetrable solidity of neatly ordered matter as just before, on the highway—it was going to be just as hard to gather evidence here. He could not fault anyone; undoubtedly they had acted reasonably, in essence not removing a thing: here were the unexpected corners, the narrow lanes and surprising thoroughfares, cobblestoned squares of greater and smaller size, a statue or fountain or a masterly combination of the two in the center, colonnaded driveways and entrances, triangular antique façades, balconies, projecting verandas and parapets standing there, timelessly, eternally, proclaiming the imperishability of the work of Spirit and Beauty—yes, everything was perfect, like an optical illusion: no crack anywhere, no room for an objection of any sort. Everything was revealed, and nevertheless everything resisted, everything was there that ought to be there, and yet everything was nevertheless false, different from how it ought to be.

He heard Hermann's question; he had probably been speaking already for minutes on end, and he wanted to know if the guest was satisfied.

"It'll do," he replied. Hermann must not be allowed to notice anything; his intent face was immediately ready to adopt an unabashed triumphalism. All at once, he now understood—and how painful the insight!—why Hermann had been willing to accompany him to the town, but no farther.

"Of course, there have been changes to one thing and another." Hermann cracked a smile.

"I see," he replied, managing to keep control of his voice, if not his feelings. If he wished to see his failure, Hermann had indubitably made a good choice of terrain; here it was in his hands, he laid down the terms. He was driving as fast as the town traffic would permit, leaving no time, no anchorage for eyes that were searching for clues—a woeful circumstance, about which he could do nothing, unless he were to betray himself and totally surrender. Fortunately, at a crossroad the traffic lights were showing red; the commissioner leaned forward, finding the crossroad suspicious, but the lamp changed to green and the car again jumped forward, so his head was thrown back by the momentum, then he again pitched forward so hard that his forehead almost knocked against the windscreen.

"Careful!" Hermann exclaimed in alarm.

"It was nothing," he assured him, though inwardly—he could sense—he was trembling all over. True, the town was not that important after all; the struggle would be decided elsewhere. Still, while that might suffice as an argument, it was no consolation: in point of fact, the inspection was starting here, and if he got nowhere with the town, what was he to count on later on? His glance was now hurriedly darting, unmethodically, from right to left, skimming up and down, flitting in spiral loops in front of the car: in vain; the expected evidence was increasingly delayed, while the car in the meantime was forging ahead and its passenger losing valuable, irrecoverable minutes.

He leaned back in the seat: it seemed he would have to give up. His eyes were smarting and dazzling from effort; he closed them in order to soothe them, his head propped on the seat's headrest, then he opened them again, just like that, with nothing in mind, simply because he already felt more rested, and then he sat up straight in astonishment. Now, just when he had been counting on nothing, there you go! All of a sudden, the town had begun to speak. What had happened? In the heat of the moment the commissioner could hardly account for it. The fault had been in the method, obviously, in the method that he had hitherto stuck to with unbending stubbornness because he had believed it to be expedient: he had been continually scanning street corners, blocks, crossroads, seeking to assemble something definite from indeterminate components, a solid entity from ephemeral details—with the logic of necessities, failure had been bound to follow. It was not that he had fallen into a trap, he had stepped into one; he could never be deceived if he himself did not err. He ought to have counted on it, and accordingly prepared for the details to be hidden in the guise of the timelessness that had been conjured up for them and of this fleeting present, this smugly mundane moment; he should have known that a purposeful gaze would glide helplessly over its slippery surface. Now though, when he had given up hoping for anything and had been running his despondent gaze aimlessly and, as it were, absent-mindedly along at the height of the uppermost story of the houses; now, purely by the aid of a prevailing impression of the angle of incident light and a color—a color that they had forgotten or been unable to change—he had, all at once, achieved his purpose. What color would that be? It radiated uniformly from every building; it was so immediate, so solid and so obvious that the commissioner almost had to think hard to remember what it was called: yellow. But could he have said anything about it? Could this conventional note-row, this abstractly empty adjective, have come close at all to this explosive yet unimaginably volatile manifestation? The commissioner gazed transfixed, spellbound—no, not gazed at it so much as gathered it in, like a fugacious scent, stalked it with all his senses and compared it, so to say, cautiously but resolutely, in order to rescue it from there and take possession of it. No doubt about it: that was the color. In that brightness of light—this color too was timeless, this too made tangible only by a mundane moment, yet a totally different moment that nevertheless could only have been hit upon in the merciless grip of this deceptive present, and for which momentarily no congruence of the map, no reconciliation of the grand total of the inventory of items, could provide requisite proof. What luck had played into his hands was precisely what he had striven to overcome by methodical work: chance—the factor that no investigation ever took into account, yet was indispensable. It was not cold calculation that he had needed, but sudden surprise; he had been searching incessantly for what had been hidden away from him, whereas he should have seized what was there to be seen. Whether he knew it or not, he had been hunting all along for what he had paid no attention: this yellow, this staggering, brutal recognition. And with this recognition, the doing of the present moment, all of a sudden the other moment that had hitherto been fruitlessly pursued had come into being, the moment the town had hidden from him and saved for him, and which could be brought into being solely through him. But see there! Everything was irrefutable, proven, and achingly certain.

Yes, that certain brightness of the sky and that certain imperial yellow. And everything that until then had held out tenaciously all of a sudden collapsed in that inexorable color and light; the solid walls became soggy as sponges; all resistance was crushed. The town became voluble in the presence of the gaze that had made it speak: it lay there before him, opening up, uncovering its pores, vanquished, still grudgingly perhaps, but already resigned. Under this gaze, it had sprung to life like a film being processed in a developer bath from the wafer-thin coat of its disguise. Its beauty had peeled off: in its place, crumbling patinas and stiff dignity stood shivering, decrepitly, senile, rendered helpless. The twining resonance of its baroque pomp—as though still straining off a bad, scratchy old record—had disintegrated, decomposed, broken up into ridiculous voices that, here and there, were still making a lonely go of it. Its decorations, streets, buildings, and ornaments were submerged in time: the mask of eternity had fallen away from them, and on display was its momentariness, the one-off randomness and hair-raising absurdity of their presence here. The commissioner looked, and he saw that the town was not the way it was shown but the way it ought to be. A mournful jubilation rose in his breast: the job was starting well, and only now did he suddenly become conscious that he was not alone. Beside him, Hermann was still talking uninterruptedly, no longer even to him, but rather behind him, to the wife, pointing his hand toward a sham-world that was deceptive, yet still demanding its existence ever more importunately, indicating, explaining: someone or other had lived here, talks were given there, from over there people had given speeches, they had governed from there; and his wife (was it out of ignorance or had their goals perhaps coincided?) was encouraging him with questions, giving audible signals of her pleasure and interest.

"Where does the bus leave from?" he interrupted rudely; the moment should not be broken, already danger threatened from all sides. Fortunately, Hermann pointed to a nearby square at the end of the street, the green boughs of its trees and the gaudily flapping awnings of its shops beckoning almost straight in front of them. First, however, they turned off suddenly into a side street. Hermann explained the maneuver as being necessitated by the traffic-control measures, and after a further turn they indeed glimpsed the square again, though this time from another angle. They came to a stop precisely at the mouth of the square; Hermann pointed out the gray buses becalmed alongside a spur of pavement opposite. They thanked him and climbed out, but the child, who had followed the sudden loss of the object of his noisy travel entertainment with alarm, now that the turn of events seemed final, angrily burst into tears in disappointment, so the wife was obliged to bend down in order to bestow on him at least the consolation of a kiss and a final tickle, and eventually, amid mutual good wishes, they said farewell. Hermann's face—the furtively relieved face of a fugitive—swiveled well-meaningly toward them from the rolled-down front-seat window to provide the excursionists with a few last-minute pieces of advice: they should have their lunch in the famous hotel that had gained its name from the rhinoceros or hippopotamus (the commissioner could clearly not have been paying sufficient attention at this point)—at any rate, a pachyderm of some sort, and if they had no objection, he suggested, he was prepared to pick them up on the way back, insofar as they considered half past four an appropriate time, in the same square. The suggestion appealed to the wife, it couldn't be dodged; yet it was questionable if he would be finished by then, and was not any defined time point merely good for cramping him? But finally they were left to themselves in the square.

"So," the woman asked, "which way now?"

"First I have to attend to my work," he replied.

"Fine," his wife said, "let's go." They walked on a few paces until they had stepped out of the deep shadow of the houses into the square, which was scorching in blazing sunlight. It was a busy square, evidently the commercially throbbing, lively heart of the artistic district; not far from the corner—opposite a domed fountain—they spotted a pastry shop, the gaily-colored sunshades, colorful tablecloths, and comfortable wickerwork chairs of its terrace enticing one to drop in. Another step or two and it was too late: the man had come to a halt.

"There's no need for you to come," he said, "if you don't want to."

"Why wouldn't I want to?" The woman gazed at him, and her frank look, her self-assured expression, all at once clouded over with foreboding.

"I'm afraid that. . ." he answered, "Well, that it will probably be very boring for you. You could take a look around town in the meantime. Then you could wait for me, let's say at this pastry shop."

The wife inspected the terrace.

"That would be even more boring," she reckoned.

"Or you could shop until then," her husband suggested.

"For what?" she asked. She did not take her unwavering look off him, and the man had to turn away in order to continue:

"I don't know. There must be something you want to buy."

"There isn't," came the answer. They fell silent. Over on the other side, there were signs of movement around the buses, as if they were preparing to leave; time was pressing, and the wife was not making things any easier.

"I need to be on my own," he burst out finally, harshly, rudely, as if he were making a confession.

"You're kidding yourself," the woman said with a shrug of her shoulders. "You can't be on your own, even you know that." Yes, he was aware of that, but he didn't wish to be aware of it; and now he saw an eddy in which the wreck of a decision, a once-proud sailing craft, was sinking, whirling languidly around, ever deeper down.

"I'm your wife," the woman carried on. They fell silent again. The man searched for words, but it was the woman who again spoke:

"I want to go with you," she said firmly, simply, in the sure knowledge of her full power.

The commissioner now stared at the pavement; he was still trying to fight but already sensed that he had lost. He knew that he had committed a careless blunder (that was what he had been worried about all along); nevertheless, he said, because he could say nothing else:

"Let's go."

They looked around at the curbside, then, hand in hand (the way they always walked together) they cut straight across the bustling road toward the buses.

## DISORIENTATION. THE GATE

On reaching the far side, the commissioner was so astounded that he had to pose to himself the question: What else had he expected? Was what surprised him, perhaps, the fact that there was not a single bus service that departed from there, with a single destination? But no one had vouchsafed to him any such information; by sober daylight even he could not have supposed that, so if he was disappointed in anything at all, it was at most in his own misapprehensions. They were standing at a run-of-the-mill bus terminus, and they had to find their own bus among five or six similar vehicles that connected the town with the surrounding countryside. Like the others, their own was a simple rural service with a practical route, a defined number of stops, at one of which—they were able to read its name among the other insignificant, meaningless place names on the dusty bus timetable—they too would have to get off: extraordinarily crafty, he concluded. The method was obviously simple-minded and transparent, yet for all that just as effective and fraught with danger. Expectation builds on monotony, the risk was of going to pieces. Would it be possible to hold out on two sticky leatherette seats that had been warmed up by the sun blazing through the closed window? Would it be possible to withstand the constant tremulous throbbing of the running motor and the passengers' desultory, soporific chatter in the enveloping fug of the bus?

Fortunately, the bus driver, who also took care of the conductor's duties (they had to buy the tickets from him), apprised them that there were just ten minutes left before departure. With a quick calculation, they found that they were unlikely to get to the location before noon, but by four-thirty Hermann would be waiting for them again, here in town; and then he had made no allowance for the wife (could he deny her lunch, a chance to cool off, a rest, relaxation?), which meant that three hours at best would be left for the inspection. He stole a glance at his wife; she was sitting mutely beside him, on her face an expression of forbearance and of endeavor not to be a burden on him. Could he hold against her the waiting and his irritation over the situation? It would be more useful to scrutinize the other passengers. They were practically all peasant men and women, with at best an occasional one, a local tradesman perhaps, of a more middle-class outward appearance. There was a conspicuously large number of florid faces criss-crossed with tangles of purple capillaries; of black headscarves, puffy backs of necks, oversized limbs, and sagging bellies and bosoms that were being carried around like extraneous baggage. They chattered stridently, alighted and reboarded, stowed their luggage up on the racks then took it down again, called over to acquaintances seated farther away in the bus, who shouted back in turn—blind instruments of a higher design, they faithfully fulfilled their roles, dutifully meeting the calculation that was attached to them. A woman in a headscarf was conveying ducklings in a basket; one of the ducklings had found access to life-giving air at the rim of the cloth covering the basket and was poking out its quacking yellow bill; without so much as looking at it, and not for a second interrupting her lively exchange of views with those seated around her, the countrywoman abstractedly pushed the loudly protesting head back into the basket with her thumb— an episode that was repeated over and over again, the ducklings and women maddeningly out-quacking one another until the bird's head was finally mercilessly tweaked and the twine knotted more tightly. His wife, a disconcerted witness to these proceedings, turned toward him several times, as if wishing to say something, but then, for some reason, had second thoughts. The violent dénouement nonetheless prompted her to express her indignation aloud, but the man responded that he had seen nothing that deviated from normal custom, at which the woman complained bitterly:

"So this is the only way, then? Are we not human beings?"

"Yes, of course. Still, we do eat ducks, after all," the commissioner replied, and his wife fell silent.

He did not really notice when they started. He had been expecting nothing worthwhile from the journey; instead he had to content himself with staying alert and guarding his attention from misleading influences that threatened him from inside and outside the vehicle alike. His wife beside him, like someone sticking to an undeclared vow, mutely endured the tension of the journey, which was reflected in her eyes and an occasional fidgety movement. There were times when he himself was unable to stifle an occasional observation that sought to be verbalized, cautiously to start with quietly, like someone not counting on anyone listening, but later on, increasingly forgetful, more animated and demanding a response, until eventually the man suddenly caught himself becoming involved in a regular conversation. He turned irritably away to the window; if they were to go on like this, the wife's quiet activity would chip away at even what meager success he had achieved in the town: her presence was placing limits on everything, constraining everything into a channel of intolerable moderation—thus the product of his mistake, the fruit of his rashness, for the sweetness of which he was already having to pay.

"Where do we get off?" the wife asked.

"I'll tell you," he replied. In any event, wherever the gradient came to an end; they had not asked anyone for more precise information, for at the start of the journey he had instantly rejected that crutch (though his wife had spoken about it with self-evident relief), so thereafter the wife had left it to him.

For the time being, however, they were still proceeding uphill, the bus puffing and panting heavily. This pain-racked and shell-pocked surface that ought to have been shaking the vehicle with the fury of bouts of fever, bouncing it on its nose, tilting it on its rear, knocking it on its side then jolting it back again, had been planed down to a smooth highway, a reliable terrain of the transport network on a hilly landscape that, while offering an undoubtedly impressive vista of the plain down below, was otherwise characterless, lacking all essentials, and could have been anywhere else. The commissioner looked with cool indifference, almost disdainfully.

All at once, they became mindful of a change: the gradient was leveling out beneath them; the bus altered speed with a huge grating, and then they slowed down as if they were approaching a stop.

The commissioner rose to his feet.

"We get off here," he said to his wife.

No one followed them; not one other passenger had any business at this deserted stop, and when the bus had moved off again, they were left on their own in the desolate scene—a welcome circumstance, by the way, which could only be good for his work.

But then, where were they? The highway there took a sweeping curve and then, barely a hundred yards farther on, dipped downward; nevertheless this hill, the place where they were standing, rendered defenseless against the lethal fire of the noonday sunshine, was still not the highest point along the ridge. All around was a barren, empty scenery, the light thrown back by white gravel to the point of being blinding; however, of the long, flat building that, by his reckoning, ought to have been on the left and farther up, with, in its center, a high-pitched roof, rising vertically to the axis of the substructure, and with the flag above all, the flag that at times like this, noon in summertime, would dangle limply on the mast-pole (whatever flag that might be, it didn't matter right now)—no trace of that was to be seen anywhere. Had they tricked him? Or had he gotten it wrong? Waiting beside him, wordless, still, patient, was his wife, while he, at this moment, which was obviously the very first moment for deeds, long-awaited action, stood there, paralyzed by helplessness, and looked around in alarm.

"What's the matter?" the woman asked timidly, which meant that the failure must already be written across his face; but was it all right to admit that, to show himself again to his wife as being weak?

"I made a mistake. I don't know which way we should go," he said.

"We'll ask someone," the woman said quietly, without any sign of surprise, stealing the magic of simple things in this absurd suggestion with her smile; and the sudden joy at not being solitary, at having a meek witness to his misery, coursed searingly through him like burning shame.

"Who?" he asked.

"Anyone. That person over there, for instance," his wife said, and pointed at a figure who was coming toward them.

Except the person had obviously not set off toward them and, if they did not accost him, would pass diagonally by them, probably heading for the bus stop.

And what a person! The commissioner looked at him with growing incredulity. He was wearing sports clothing, clothes patterned from head to toe with a check of large squares, a jacket and plus fours, boots and woolen socks in this heat, with on his head a peaked cloth cap of the same checkered material. He was striding as if walking on stilts, wading with self-assured caution in some familiar swamp; on his long nose were gold-framed spectacles and his ready smile revealed a set of pure gold teeth.

How had he come to appear before them in this deserted bit of countryside, and at the very moment when there was a need for him? Was he a pilgrim or an inhabitant of the district? Reality or a dream-figure? The commissioner could only guess.

In any event, here he was and speaking, so there was no doubting his reality. "Certainly, pleased to set you straight, no trouble," he said, his eyes gleaming, and stretched out a long arm with a big bony hand at the end in precisely the opposite direction to that which the commissioner's calculations indicated. They were looking for the area's sights, were they? Just keep on in that direction, but hurry, the program would be starting soon: there was a cinema there and a museum, historical ruins and modern works of art, sideshows for the living, repose for the dead—a varied and instructive program, which had guaranteed schedules, timed down to the minute, every one with an expert lecturer or guide.

"What's that? . . . What are you talking about?" The commissioner was astounded.

"But that's how it is," the man smiled.

"Have you been there, by any chance?" He switched to interrogation.

"More than once," came the proud answer.

"But why?" He aimed the question at him.

"I live here, not far away. I'm on my own, so what am I supposed to do with my Sundays?" The man he was facing looked at him with a piercing, almost reproachful gaze.

"Let's go!" the commissioner said, grasping his wife by the arm and wheeling her in the direction that had been designated. The man was plainly a lunatic, or if not a lunatic, then possibly a rascal, not that it mattered: they would soon see if he had been telling the truth.

They had only a few steps to go in order to reach the crest of the truncated cone that was the hill. They were greeted by a light breeze to cool off their hot brows, making the commissioner smile involuntarily (that being how one is supposed to reciprocate expected greetings) before breathing in deeply, an intense look on his face, like a connoisseur assessing the aroma of a vintage wine. He could not work undisturbed. An unbearable brilliance flashed in his eyes: rays of sunlight were performing an infuriating dance in the distance on half a dozen or more shells of metal and glass. Could those be coaches? They were, idly beached and evidently empty, awaiting their absent passengers. They could in no way belong to the fleet of the local service, the gray shabbiness of which would be put to shame next to these industrial masterworks of blue, red, yellow, green, and brown, one and another of which boasted upper decks and air-conditioning, and even the most modest of which flaunted some eye-catching company logo on its side, cajoling travelers with the strident offerings of tour operators. The commissioner stepped closer in order to see them better: he read the names of cities and countries near and far, from all quarters of the globe. The blow was unforeseen: he had not counted on having to deal with tourists, though on thinking it over, and even ignoring the man's words just before, was it not his own fault if precisely this circumstance had found him unready? Tourists were like ants, diligently carrying off the significance of things, crumb by crumb, wearing away a bit of the unspoken importance investing them with every word they spoke and every single snapshot they took. He should have realized that this was precisely the sort of opportunity they would not leave unexploited. Where could they be? he wondered, looking around with morose curiosity: Did this happen to be an interval in operations or, on the contrary, were the shows in full swing for them somewhere? It was impossible to tell; they were nowhere to be seen, only the mute threat of the deserted coaches was there to be sued for ownership rights of this bleak locality.

He became aware that his wife was calling. Just beforehand, in his haste, he had left her behind, and it was from there that she was calling. She was pointing something out, and the commissioner turned around in order to follow her upraised arm.

"Look, a gate!" the wife said.

Yes. Over there, on the spine, on the boundary between the ground and nothingness, where the escarpment came to an end and the imagination suspected a chasm, a two-winged gatehouse rose solitarily into the sky.

The commissioner set off toward it with restrained deliberateness, as if his caution were setting the scale of hope: Was that the gate?

It could be; why not, after all? The lie of the land, this privileged point on the crooked slope would make it very suitable indeed to be that. One undoubtedly had to entertain that surmise—but without this hammering of the heart, which threw itself like a maniac at every chance, however unproven, carrying rational sense off on the wrong track: the gate should be bigger. This gate here was small, insignificant, a trifle; it vanished in the surroundings, it was all but ludicrous. And the wrought-iron decoration on the two pierced wings—those patterns! The scrolls! The intricate texture, the iron braiding, the hinges, the ornaments that were so complex, impenetrable, crossing and intertwining like the gangways of fate—where were they? The design of this ornamentation here was so simple that it had no aspect that could not be comprehended at the first glance: rhombuses, plain ordinary wrought-iron rhombuses cut up into parallel rows by straight vertical bars, double welds at the joints—no question that it was first-rate work, but far from the artistically polished craftsmanship that it ought to be. Yet it was the gate, for all that, without a shadow of doubt.

"I can see some sort of writing in the middle," his wife informed him, but they were standing too far away to make out the three units—presumably three words—into which the inscription, which, being imbedded in the center of the gate's pattern, looked from there to be merely one of its curlicues. "J . . . j-e . . ." she tried to spell it out.

"*Jedem das Seine*. To each his due," the commissioner helped her out.

The woman fell silent, turned her head to one side and bowed it—like an ashamed child who had been given a sudden dressing-down in the midst of its self-absorbed games.

"Odd," she said quietly.

"Certainly," the commissioner smiled. "Obviously odd for some. But it contains a truth that is well worth consideration; you just have to decipher it," he added.

His wife cast a searching look at him.

"Does that apply to us too?" she asked.

The man kept silent.

"You're holding me up," he said eventually. "I have to go."

He rushed on, and with his long strides was there at the gate in no time at all.

"I have to see," he muttered.

But the person for whom he intended this hasty, apologetic explanation, his wife, was no longer beside him. He turned round to see her standing alone in the place where the two of them had been just before. She had not made a single step after him, had not budged an inch to catch up; she was merely following him with her eyes, which seemed worn in the futile struggle with the blinding sunshine. She had raised an elbow over her brow in an attempt to seek shelter against it in the thin, fallible shadow of her forearm; her figure was already made smaller by the distance and the immeasurable perspective of the emptiness down below. The commissioner surrendered himself for a minute to the unnameable anguish that emanated from this painful spectacle. What more could he do for his wife? He cupped the palms of his hands around his mouth:

"I'll be back!" he shouted over to her from the barred background of the gate.

The woman's face seemed practically to contort from the effort of shouting back:

"When?" Her voice rose up to him, awakening a strange feeling in the commissioner, the astounding sense of a sort of dreamlike realization. That was precisely the question that was supposed to be heard, and melting away just as feebly in space, yet multiplied in the same way from the echo as if—yes—that question was not even his, but she had simply shouted it out, thereby, as it were, breathing life into the mute souls of each and every question in this area with her live voice, and he all but shuddered as it occurred to him that it was now his turn to give an answer to her.

"The next bus leaves in an hour and a half!" he yelled.

What sort of feebleness had seized hold of him? Why had he submitted to a demand that had not even been made? He spun on his heels, almost surprised at himself: enough, he had already sacrificed a lot for the wife as things were, much too much, so now that he had hobbled himself in the fetters of time for her sake, not a moment was to be lost.

## ASTONISHMENT. INSPECTION. HOSTELRY

He set off straight toward the gate, but he had not even started before he was stopping short. Something he ought to have seen all along but, it seemed, had been overlooked as being of minor importance was now, all at once, looming before him like a cast-iron fact, with the stubborn resistance of its materiality: the gate was locked. He was clearly going to have to revise his original plan of stepping onto the scene of his task by passing under it; the commissioner was boiling mad. So they were forcing him to take a detour? He was to sneak in furtively, by some back entrance, into a place that he should be entering with head held high, like a conqueror? He was almost of a mind to fly at the gate, to push or force it, to overcome this evil and ever-renewed resistance on the part of things, but then sober reason soon gained the upper hand.

He was still roughly two or three steps away from the gate—a few steps that would have to be taken on an upward slope. As yet, therefore, he could not see what was beyond the gate, since that was where the slope switched downward. Yet in struggling with the gate, would he be able to withstand the temptation to take at least a single peek behind it, thereby endangering the result, the goal, the entire huge expectation that he had pinned on that sight?

Therefore, he set off on a path, or rather not a path but more a remembrance of footsteps on the ground, a threshold; it led on past the remains of an aged, fraying barbed-wire fence, maintenance of which had visibly been neglected, leaving time to erode and blacken it. The commissioner gently touched its rust-eaten, crumbling spikes with his fingertips: a smart way to start, he concluded. A person might almost feel in the mood to stop and dutifully muse on this image of decay—were he not aware, of course, that this was precisely the goal; that the play of ephemerality was merely a bait for things. A well-chosen trap, at all events, an ingenious idea: What else was he going to have to contend with, he wondered? He should not rush anything. This time he was independent; there was no one to impose inhibitory conditions; he himself would lay down the law on his task, he alone would answer for his mistakes and his results. Here another method was needed than down below, in the town. Here it was not a case of getting the place to speak, but quite the reverse: he would be the touchstone for the place, it was he himself who had to speak. To become an instrument, so that his sounding should be the signal. Yes, this time it was not a matter of him having to expose the sight, but of him having to expose himself to the sight; not of collecting evidence but of becoming the proof, a contrite yet implacable witness to the victory that would pulse up as proof.

In a few more paces the barbed-wire fence snapped, so he should turn left there in order to see. He stopped in order to check himself: yes, it was unnecessary to take out the sketch-map of the area (he had it stowed in a pocket, ready for any eventuality). All the preparations, measurements, checking, and reconciling had done their bit; he knew exactly what he should be seeing; the whole spectacle lay before his eyes in its outlines, its every nook, space, each and every building, barrack, and alley. He didn't have to do anything, just check what was known and then surrender himself to that knowledge.

He swung round, and on that most favorable point on the hill, whence the broad-winged soaring of the vista opened out, he let his gaze run freely, like a hunter his hawk, and from what he saw he became almost rooted to the spot.

Below him was spread an empty field, a windswept, grass-covered, bare hillside that stretched out from his feet all the way to a wreath that turned into the arc of a distant, darker strip of forest.

What had done this? Nature, or destruction wrought by human hands? No, nature alone did not carry out such perfect work. The commissioner looked disconcertedly around. Nothing anywhere, just this clean vale, its green inviting one to stroll—yes, perfect work, even if the perfection in itself was revealing of the anguished motive that had obviously given rise to it. This time they had not been satisfied with any inclination to yield; they had trusted nothing to pure appearance, left nothing to chance, in the labyrinth of natural decay and abyssal connections. And had they not achieved the goal? Was this place not already giving rise to doubt? The commissioner was seized, for the first time in the course of his trip, by a presentiment of defeat, like the numb stupor of fraught and arduous dreams.

What should he cling on to for proof? What was he to fight with, if they were depriving him of every object of the struggle? Against what was he to try and resist, if nothing was resisting? He had prepared for a fight and had come upon a deserted battleground. It was not an enemy, but the lack of an enemy, that was forcing him to lay down arms . . .

Moving human shapes separated out densely from the dazzling background. The commissioner jerked his head that way in exasperation: there were figures approaching him from the right. Who was that woman with the goose neck? Her tiny, prematurely aged face a shriveled fruit in the drying-room of injured sedulousness, even from afar already waving her arms around in protest, like a flail. What did that gray uniform and faded necktie signify? A representative of the supervisory authority, an attendant, girl guide leader, a cemetery guard? And who was that immobile other person behind her, a mute shadow towering on a more distant bluff, in that almost ankle-length black dress, a wind-buffeted mourning veil over her face, a black specter in the light's azure and gold—an antique incubus, Antigone, with merely a smoke-smudged, cold, hard, bleak, and sober tracery in the distance, behind her back, instead of the noble columns of Thebes?

The uniformed woman was already standing there in front of him. The commissioner could not make out what she was saying. All he understood in his flash of astonishment, face to face with this brutally undisguised spectacle of betrayal and treachery, was that someone was seeking to get in his way, to impose a fresh obstacle on his work, to prevent him getting any farther. Did they take him for an unauthorized intruder? A tourist who had strayed from the flock? He said something to her, he himself didn't know what, but he sensed that his voice was echoing over the scene, that his words were capable of breaking through floodgates, or of holding back great rivers. He hurled in her face his identity and the full force of his quivering anger.

How the woman had shut up! How she had scooted out of sight! He must have looked awesome in her eyes to have had that effect. Meager recompense, though, for what would he gain by it?

He set off down the slope, transversely across the meadow, though he was unclear where he was going and for what purpose. His feet carried him at an ever brisker pace. He cut over the pasture, loping like a hound that has lost the trail, following nonexistent scents toward imaginary quarries; and he experienced nothing other than the persistently meek and unassailably malevolent patience of landscapes, hillsides, and open country. He became entangled in knee-high grass, struggled in weed-overgrown tracts, the soil of a gravelly clearing crunched under his shoes; flower stalks quivered from the leaps of grasshoppers, butterflies performed their summer dance in front of him, while over there, above the forest, a rapacious hawk was hovering on the lookout for prey. A displaced sense of implausibility gradually took hold of the commissioner. Had he blundered into the wrong place? If nothing at all that was supposed to be here was here, then maybe every previous assumption had been mistaken, every piece of evidence false and abstract. Then this place was not what it was either, just his own stubborn obsession. Then he himself was not who he was, either, and his mission was an error. Space, time, the ground beneath his feet—nothing was true. Then there was no other truth either, only this irresistible impulse, constantly assailing every sensory organ: this stillness and the summery tranquility of this gentle valley. Yes, in which case he would have to terminate his assignment and accept this one and only true and tangible offer, the intoxicating gold of this blazing summer, just like the lizards scurrying around his feet that his steps had disturbed from the sun-basking peace of their happy present.

He set off back up toward the hill from which he had reached there. Should he accept failure? Make do with the hostile certainty of the lizards and insects, the scenery and things, the sun and sky, even his own senses, his incontrovertible body: his lead-weighted legs, his burning eyes, his blanking-out brain? Yes, was it not possible that he himself, who was anyway prone to this temptation, was also an enemy? . . . The commissioner looked around: What more could he try? Over there, higher up, black shadows were speckling, lines streaking the green terrain. Tourists? Had they perhaps finished one item on the program and another was just about to start? He saw farther off a lonely, pavilion-like building; the column was headed that way. Like a submissive flock, they were proceeding wherever they were driven, their carefree chattering had already roused the sleeping landscape.

The commissioner set off toward them; by quickening his pace it proved a childishly simple task to mingle with them. He reached a room, an exhibition hall: What could this be? It was as if he had strayed into an aquarium amid the finds of dead monsters, stuffed dragons, and fossils. The exhibition hall still reeked of fresh paint, everything cheerfully illuminated, cordoned off, slapped behind panes of glass, and in this confidence-inspiring environment of surpassing orderliness, scientific preparations, and discreet abstraction a strange, albeit not exactly shameful subject matter was on display: the props of horror novels, a market stock of squalid dreams, a collection of defunct implements of past ages, an assortment of contraband curiosities. He looked and recognized nothing. What could this collection of junk, so cleverly, indeed all too cleverly disguised as dusty museum material, prove to him, or to anyone else for that matter? Its objects could be brought to life only by being utilized. The only test of their efficacy could be experience, and even here there was no other truth than this crowd and the stuffiness of the room. But then, had they crammed big enough throngs in here, and was this room stifling enough? And how leisurely this fastidious multitude was moving around here, in this regulated milieu: on their faces was an expression of moderate curiosity in a predictable adventure on which they had embarked out of rashness and boredom. They were nodding, looking around; some things took their fancy and others they swung away from and moved on.

He had no business here. Out of here! Out, into the at least silent and inward-looking negation of sunlight and stubborn landscape. He had to push through a further throng of people waiting outside, press into the warmth of bodies, catching whiffs of tobacco and perfume, his ears assailed by a babble of chatterers. He elbowed his way through them, and their din accompanied him to the top of the hill.

It was still early. On his way here he would have thought even three hours too little for his task; then he had restricted himself to an hour and a half, and in the end even that had proved too much—and his wife was nowhere to be seen. He set off on a light stroll in the vicinity—unmarked, unforthcoming paths carried him on their backs with the mute indifference of pack animals that convey their burdens yet retain the memory of no load. What temptation was attracting his look over there, in a soft crook of the undulating countryside, in a ring of parked cars? It was a new building that they had manifestly conjured up for the square not long ago and wasted no time in bringing about: a hostelry? Why not? The commissioner was not even surprised. This brazenness was at least charming, and in any event did not hide what was on offer. He approached at a leisurely pace. On the inn-sign they were promising excellent beer, iced refreshing drinks, cold and warm snacks—undoubtedly a useful establishment, the demand on which it was founded being as ruthless as the innocence of children.

He entered and stopped near the door, in the manner of a guest searching for a place, in order to take stock of the operation. The premises were packed, the tables occupied; bustling waiters forced their way through carrying heavy dishes and bubbling drinks. His attention was arrested by a noisy company: a group of men was seated around a table, before them the remains of finished meals and a mass of glasses, empty or full. These weren't tourists, one could see that right away, or if they were, then not ordinary ones. They were sitting there manifestly at home, as if claiming proprietary rights to the place, yet somehow strangely ill at ease—he recognized them, you bet he did! They were the ones, yes, unknown acquaintances who were just as much haunted by a compulsion to revisit in the way that we always yearn to see tormenting dreams again, perhaps in the secret hope that a time will even come when we understand them. . . . Had they been successful, he wondered, or had they failed? Had they installed themselves here to celebrate, or to forget? It would be interesting to find out from them. His gaze went from face to face, and they must have sensed this covetous presence, because all of a sudden they fell silent and—almost as a sign of the instincts stirring even in the depths of their stupor—took a good look at the new guest before again turning to one another. The commissioner was veritably shaken by his eerie power, having identified himself, to join them at their table.

But what would be gained by that? Should he give away his work, complete his failure? Try to share with them something that could not be shared? Persuade himself that he was not alone? No, that solution was kept for the more fortunate. The game may have been lost, but it went on; he could not relinquish his assignment yet. Yes, he thought wryly to himself, the losses have not yet come to an end.

Without signaling, he slipped out of the door and made a beeline for the bus, where his wife was probably waiting for him.

## THE PALM COURT. THE VEILED WOMAN

He got there at the right moment: he and his wife had hardly greeted each other when the bus loomed on the bend of the highway, so that the question that had been, as it were, hovering on the wife's lips was left hanging. Fortunately, the grinding noise (the driver was obviously applying the brakes on the downward section of the route) drowned out all other sounds, so that there was no chance for conversation during the journey—but then, what could he have said? He had no right to enlighten his wife; he could not belie the seriousness of her look, turn it against himself; he could not ask what was the meaning of those scant few meadow flowers in her lap that she was perhaps taking home to preserve as a devotional object of her mute alliance, or where she had been while he conducted his inspection, what he had been convinced of, what trap he had been led into, and what sort of appearances he had fallen prey to. A revolt of forbearance was the sole disdainful answer that could be given to the provocative ridicule of the hard facts; he had to protect his secret, the responsibility—this consuming emptiness—was his alone to carry.

Why, instead of gratitude, did he feel the irritation of an ill-tempered resentment if he saw the wife assisting him with mute compliance? That was a senseless question that now would only deflect him from his work.

He helped his wife down from the vehicle. They saw their square again; the noon traffic was bustling on the melting asphalt. They decided to have lunch; they were hungry. A brief consultation took place between them over the direction—both of them quoted Hermann's instructions and it became clear they had interpreted them differently—until they left it to the gaps and paths opening up amid miniature palaces, dreaming squares, parks with clipped hedges and dozily sun-drenched osier-beds, as if they had confidence that, in the end, their appetite would help them to their goal.

There could be no mistaking it: this proud façade, this weathered revolving door, this betasseled and epauletted doorman, half serious, half comic in his finery, could not be deceiving them. A nod of the head was the greeting for cronies, a stretching-out of his arm an invitation for kings into an enchanted realm. They cut across a dingy anteroom, their feet sinking into thick carpets, all around the spell of sparklingly lacquered little tables and soft draperies, like the song of mute sirens calling on those who know how to die happy to run aground in these luxurious shallows. They were received at the entrance to the restaurant by the maître d'hôtel; they were handed on to a waiter in tails, who led them—unexpected high seas—into the palm court. Selection of a menu was a ceremony of the devious sounding-out of the initiated, of guardedly concealed questions and replies of a magic power which dispelled all doubts and led to flitting obligingness without reservation. He was immersed in a world of cut-glass goblets, silver cutlery, and quality porcelain; lulled by distinguished smiles and hushed, multilingual talk; surrounded by slight clinking, wafting odors, the ever-changing curls of cigarette smoke, coiling like sluggish sea animals; entranced by the foaming and fizzing drinks and the light steam slipping by the sparkling glasses with the gentleness of sudden emotion; carried along by the liberated delight of his own body at the stimulus of tastes in a blind adventure of alimentation—the commissioner sat distractedly in the depths of this green murk, in the dreamy languor of someone replete with lotus-eating. Where was his work? Did it still exist at all?

Relaxed and sitting back, crowning their stupor with aromatic tobacco, these two exiles from the victoriously reigning present now weighed up the possibilities for further passing the time. The wife proposed a walk. Confronting her with her pronouncements of the previous day, he asked her to account for the change in the expectations she attached to the town. In this well-timed demand he was seized by the temptation to redeem this truncated day, fraught as it had been by disruptions, with a shared experience of self-abandoned delectation; this vacillating moment, in which every conviction seemed doubtful, offered no counterargument.

They paid the bill, the brutal act being mitigated by the intimacy of the procedure, tactful aversions of gaze and placatory smiles. Again they contended with the soft comfort of the anteroom. While the wife went to the restroom with her handbag of beauty preparations, in order to freshen up, the man eyed an invitingly deep armchair.

What was to stop him from throwing himself into it and spreading himself out with a yawn? Angry shame that would burn through even the sluggishness of digestion? Or maybe that female figure in the dark dress who was gliding noiselessly toward him, from somewhere on the soft carpet, until she was standing before him, probably mustering him with her enigmatically burning gaze from behind that mourning veil?

How had she gotten here? Had he preceded her or maybe followed her? Why did she not speak?

"Madam?" he said in the end, not knowing himself how he had lighted on this semi-interrogative, semi-distancing, old-fashioned mode of address.

"Sir?" the locution was returned in similar currency by a deep-sounding female voice, and the veil seemed to flutter as though from suppressed laughter.

"Can I do anything for you?" the commissioner asked.

"What can anyone do for me?" the woman responded. "I saw you up on top," she added.

"On top?" the commissioner asked uncertainly.

"You chased off that woman inspector. You spoke about your assignment. What did you accomplish?" The commissioner flinched at the implacability of her voice.

"On what ground are you asking me?" he asked, more sharply than he had intended.

"On what ground would you keep it to yourself?" the woman riposted, no less rudely.

"I don't know who you are, madam," the commissioner said disconcertedly.

"Nor do I any longer," came the answer. The veiled face moved, turning slightly sideways from him. "My father," she said slowly, leaving a pause between each and every word. "My younger brother. My fiancé."

"I'm terribly sorry," said the commissioner. "I can't be of any help."

The veil again turned to face him.

"My father, my younger brother, and my fiancé," the woman repeated, as if she had heard nothing.

"I have done everything that I can do," said the commissioner. "You can't accuse me of anything."

"You misunderstand me," the woman answered. "How could I accuse you? There is no charge that you could not refute. After all, you are here."

"By chance," said the commissioner.

"There's no such thing as chance," he heard dully and tremulously from behind the veil. "Only injustice."

There was a pause, there being no answer to that assertion. What did he have to prove the opposite? And was a credible witness to be found who would be able to prove it?

"The reason I am here is to try to redress that injustice," he said after all, softly, almost like someone apologizing.

"Redress . . . ? How? With what?"

The commissioner all at once found the words he wanted, as if he could see them written down: "So that I should bear witness to everything I have seen." Then he added, slightly plaintively, as if he were only thinking aloud, "I would not have credited that my work here would be made so much more difficult."

"Perhaps it's you who's making it more difficult: you surround yourself with too many reliefs," was the rejoinder to that.

"What are you thinking of?" the commissioner asked.

"What's your wife doing here?"

Though it was as if he had already counted on that question, the commissioner was nevertheless overcome by weakness, as if he had suddenly become defenseless. "You're silent. I'll credit you with that, at any rate," the woman concluded. She raised her hand to the veil and pulled it aside with an easy movement, so the commissioner was confronted with a face—except it was no longer a face but a yellow, desiccated, petrified simulacrum of a face. Only the reflection of some consuming inner incandescence gave life to that mask, a wordless and insatiable calling to account now became fixed on it; an all-engulfing demand, like a monument to implacability.

The commissioner turned away in repulsion.

"No," he said. "I have done everything. Everything. You can't ask more of me than I am capable of. What more do you want? There are limits to what I can do . . . the scale of my powers . . . I too have rights!" he almost shouted.

"Well then, exercise them!" he heard the organ peal of the voice, and by the time he had turned round and set off after her—to detain her? Appease her?—he found himself face to face only with the smile of his wife as she was coming back.

"What happened?" the wife asked.

"Nothing," he replied. "Although," he added, "we're going to have to modify the program." And he was left an unwilling spectator as an animated face was extinguished and a smile was wiped out.

## RUSH HOUR

They no longer looked where they were going. The number of people on the pavements multiplied, they were jostled in an ever-growing swarm. A group pushing the other way split them up from one another and, by the time the commissioner had fought his way through them, his wife was nowhere to be seen. In the end, though, he spotted her a few steps behind, standing with some anciently bound book in hand, amid the merchandise of a bookshop, which was set out in boxes, on revolving stands, even on the pavement itself.

"Iphigenia in Tauris." She flashed a smile up at him, just as she was stooping down to replace the book in the box from which she had evidently taken it beforehand.

"Long-windedness dressed up as classicism, tawdry romanticism," the commissioner dismissed it.

"I wouldn't say that," said the wife. "When I was a student I was very fond of it for some reason. Now I've even forgotten what it's about."

"Good thing too," said the commissioner. "Cheating and lies set in blank verse."

"That's not how I remember it," the wife protested. "There was a love story in it . . . " She pondered a little. "A man renounces the girl he is in love with," he said. "For the sake of nobler principles," she added.

"That goes without saying," said her husband. "In chronicle plays, country bumpkins like that are always ennobled."

"I remember now," —the wife's voice grew excited— "She was a priestess, but in reality the prisoner of a barbarian king on a peninsula."

"On Tauris," muttered the commissioner.

"How did she come to be there?" His wife looked at him.

"Because Daddy, the great military leader, for the sake of procuring favorable winds for his fleet, was prepared to sacrifice his favorite daughter to the goddess Artemis. But the goddess merrily whisked the girl away from the very midst of the already crackling flames, straight to Tauris."

"Dreadful tale," said the wife.

"Pretty depressing," her husband agreed. "And when she got there an even crueler fate awaited her: in the services of the evil ceremonies of a barbarian deity, she was supposed to slit the throats of all strange men captured by the barbarian inhabitants."

"Yes, indeed, but as I recall it she managed, over time, to tone down the ceremony by persuading the king that she should only murder the prisoners symbolically, not in reality."

"Just like that," the commissioner declared abstractedly.

"But what I liked was the climax of the story," his wife carried on. "The scene where her brother comes to get her, to release her from the king and take her home. A small band lands on the coast in secret; the brother and sister recognize each other . . . if I'm not mistaken, the girl doesn't want to go away with them at first, because she feels it's shameful to leave the king by furtively running away . . . "

"A minor detail," the man said, shrugging. "The point is, the king learns that the borders of his kingdom have been violated and, heading an armed squad, he surprises them on the beach. On top of everything else, they also want to steal from his temple."

"They could not have seen that as stealing: they wanted to restore their own devotional article, the statue of the goddess, to its proper place."

"In the spirit of the local legal codes, at any rate, that amounted to stealing," the man noted.

"Fair enough." His wife let it pass. "So the king had a twofold ground for revenge. Instead of that, however, he gradually yields to the force of the priestess's arguments and renounces not only revenge but love as well. He lets her go; indeed, even gives them a present."

Since the man remained silent, she asked, "Wasn't that what happened?"

"That is what they want us to believe, at any rate," he responded.

The swarm around them had meanwhile continued to grow; they had to step out of people's way and people had to step out of their way, until the streets again, all at once, opened out and they found themselves once again in the already familiar square. In the thick of rushing people and vehicles, their legs carried them involuntarily to the sanctuary of the terrace of the confectioner's shop. A table with two easy chairs was standing unoccupied in the corner, giving a comfortable view, like a theatre box, of the pavement and a monotonously splashing, cone-shaped fountain. They took seats.

"So how did it happen?" the wife asked.

"Differently," the man said, lighting a cigarette, then asking the white-bonneted waitress who had just stepped up for iced drinks.

"How?" the wife asked again.

"How. . .?" The commissioner seemed to hesitate for a moment. "Well all right, if you're so interested," he tacked on. "Briefly, the troops in the squad surrounded the men, then they attacked them, disarmed them, and shackled them. Next, before the eyes of the menfolk, the troops violated the priestess, after which, before the eyes of the priestess, the men were hacked to pieces. Then they looked to the king, and he waited until he spotted on the priestess's face the indifference of misery that cannot be exacerbated any further. He then gave the signal for mercy to be exercised, and his troops finally gave her too the coup de grace ... oh, and not to forget! That evening they all went to the theatre to watch the barbarian king exercising clemency on the stage as they, snug in the dress circle, sniggered up their sleeves."

They fell silent.

"You're being unfair," the wife said after a while, in a quiet and seemingly weary voice.

"No doubt," the commissioner replied, as if he were slightly ashamed. "I can't be fair," he added, already more abstractedly.

His attention was at that moment—indeed had been for several minutes now—engaged by something else. His gaze was roving about the street, first wandering along the pavement, then sweeping over the entire big square, which was chopped up by a four-lane roadway, a traffic intersection, complicated obstructions, a roundabout detour, the islands of bus stops. What was going on here before his eyes? To begin with, he sought the answer in vain; in this confused moment, rent by noise, rumbling, rattling, piercingly flashing shards of light and thundering, all he could have accounted for were a sinister, as yet confusedly hazy presentiment of an impending incident and his own ever-growing excitement. What was he anticipating? What lay in wait? What he would witness, indeed maybe even participate in? He didn't know. He sat mutely in his place, a hand resting on the table, his cigarette trembling slightly between his fingers. The tension was mounting. What before had been merely an inchoate anxiety was now searing his chest with the white heat of anguish. All his sensory organs were on standby, collecting impressions, picking up signals, although he was hardly in a position to interpret those signals. What could he do here? He looked around and could not help seeing how everything was ganging up on him; appraise this perhaps unwitting yet, all the same, cruelly precise intertwining of however many circumstances were turning against him. Impossible, it seemed, to stymie anything, to avert a process that was perceptibly unfolding more and more and obviously threatening catastrophe, or even, at least, just to sort out its connections with a clear head.

In front of their theatre box—this island that was proving steadfast, for the time being, in the eddying commotion—happened to be a stop on the town's bus route. Vehicles would pull in and push off on their way, practically one after the other. They discharged billows of humanity helter-skelter from their open-flung doors, then sucked them in again, like great beasts performing their metabolic processes. The people spilling out had to vie with those striving to get on, then, on the ground, they dispersed to swell the heaving surge of the ever-increasingly raging tide of the street. People and vehicles streamed endlessly; each and every outlet of the square seemed to be a bottomless sack, the inexhaustible contents of which were being released at storm force. Yes, the swish of lashing commands and whips would drive them to this square, now—so it seemed—everybody was gathering here from the four corners of the town (or was it maybe the whole world?).

He became mindful of a young man who was standing there, one hip propped against the rail around the terrace, a motionless point in the seething morass of motion. An incongruous moustache on his serious face; his hair tumbling to his shoulders in out-fanning tresses. His transfigured, silky wisp of a beard showed him to be a saint; the fur-trimmed jacket, to be a trendy follower of fashion. He had just lifted his hand in order to adjust something, tug it into place. It may have been that movement that had attracted attention to him; that long, never-still, nervous hand that was now, middle finger flexed, nevertheless resting for a minute on his chest. The commissioner was seized by an odd sensation, an uncertainty in regard to time and his own whereabouts, a sense of déjà vu: he had seen that gesture, that face, that young man, somewhere before, if not in real life then maybe in a film, a photograph, possibly a painting. What came to mind, though he himself was not clear through what associations of thought, were his own words, which he had come across hardly an hour before as if he were seeing them in print, while about the words one name, then another, that of the artist who, sometime long, long ago, had roamed this way and, in a series of engravings, bore witness to everything he had seen...

He was seized by a sudden anxiety, for in the whirl of motions and movements he seemed to have lost track of the man—but no, there he was, standing where he had been before, propped against the rail, right now watching the street, and then, a bit later, turning his face this way, the face of the young Albrecht Dürer: a painting was coming to life before his very eyes, and at one and the same time the artist himself. More specifically, the painter's portrait of his own face, framed in the fur-trimmed collar of his coat. Was this a vision or blind chance? Where had this man sprung from? He had not seen him arrive, and now he was standing there, almost right next to him, with the taciturn self-confidence of someone for whom this watch-post was his eternal home in this commotion.

What could he be looking at? It was not possible to gather from the enigmatic, gloomy expression of that irregular pair of eyes, which had undoubtedly already scrutinized people and was nevertheless still scrutinizing them, ever more closely, with the melancholy obstinacy of an artist or a pickpocket. He turned away from him in order to be able to make out the direction of his gaze, which was cast nowhere in particular yet was all-seeing. All at once, everything fell into place; the jerkily spinning series of scenes was at once filled with sense. He saw him just the way he had seen the town in the morning.

The square expanded, its center sinking, its perspectives collapsing, so that the hill crest he had traversed that morning, which just before had merely been hazily visible in the distance, now seemed to be growing directly out of the square's end. The sky opened up in the midst of the blinding flash of sputtering refractions of light, and in the flood of flames and sparks from the pitiless sun—intensified to a fever pitch by a thousand metallic objects, chromium, panes of glass, tiled roofs—it made ready to come crashing down. Was the horn still singing in its seven corners the grief of the cars, or were they the trumpets of the Dies Irae sounding? The fountain across the street, like a huge mamma that had been wrung by two pitiless hands and transformed it into a spouting volcanic crater that, rattling, whistling, with helplessly twitching spasms, spat out its turbid contents. Yes, this was no longer a square but a vale of tears. Several people were getting up, horrified, from their places on the terrace in order to view the horror: everything had become stuck in the rush-hour traffic and was milling in a single narrow, indescribably busy circle. The street resembled a river on which everything had come to a stop, become clogged; every ship had sprung a leak, and all hands on board were fighting for air, for their existence. From one car, its top back, two arms thrust up to the sky rose aloft among the wrecks rolling about in the spume of the sea swell, as if a passenger on a sinking boat were giving a final wave.

The situation was even grimmer here, on dry land (the pavement). People were mingling, bumping into one another, stumbling, desperately seeking support with flailing arms in the burgeoning cacophony, below a sun that was blazing angrily down on them. And what faces the maelstrom was casting up and dragging down! They were all bobbing around here: fat ones, thin ones, the broken, the hopeful, the all-suspecting, branded with the sign of their fate, the underhand, the pushy ones who were confident of finding their own way out. In the frenzy, however, they were all the same. What could differences in their ages, fates, lives, or passions signify here? This shared fate, which had gathered all life here, unified them in the bottleneck of this shared battle; it would tolerate nothing else here, apart from the shared passion of the moment; thus, it silenced and brushed off from them all stray, fugitive sensation of their personal existence, as though it were the ruthless command of all-powerful dictators, or the maniacal will of great creators, coercing their frescoes under the stamp of a sole thought, without losing sight of the tiniest detail in the clear-sighted madness of the exercise of their rule . . .

Yes, every face here spoke, or preached, about one thing, demanded one thing, pleaded for one thing, professed a single doctrine: "Get out of here!" That was what was said by the face of that elderly, bald man over there, even if his strength ran to no more than simply closing his eyes and hiding his horror-stricken face in his hands. Or that mother with the hunted look, who—in hope of what kind of grace, one wondered—was compulsively fumbling with her child's clothing to bare its body. And that prematurely aged boy, who seemed to have grown up all at once under an incomprehensible terror and, lips crumpled, sobbing shrilly, was relieving himself by the curbside. Who could have been thinking of themselves here? And where was there anybody who was not thinking of themselves? Exhausted and throwing in the towel; cursing; or resignedly, simply accepting it as sheer blind fate; patiently holding one's ground, registering every shove, kick, and blow out of some wise foresight, as it were, some bitter experience; carrying or being carried along, stumbling or riding roughshod over others—they were all just serving the law of the maelstrom. There were those who became so immersed in the orgy of shared passion, like that female head over there, almost swimming among the others on her disengaged, dislocated neck: the woman's sunken face and her gaping mouth those of the damned, her flaming hair like a scream, the pain in her narcotized, vacant expression no longer distinguishable from some deranged pleasure in being lost.

But what was happening over there? With rolling steps, a woman crosses the multitude as it opens up before her legs. For a minute, everything comes to a halt and all hurry is forgotten. Was this parting throng giving way before a queen? Looks from all sides are fastened on her; looks hoping for redemption, ease-ment, or at least the fleeting diversion of an unexpect-ed flicker of solace in the consuming scramble; looks that all want to make her their own and yet, in the end, all meeting in this shared hope, making their shared target the shared property of a shared hope. Everyone turns round in her wake: men, old bats, young people, husbands with wives on their arms, and the wives themselves. Enchanting everyone as she proceeded to run the gauntlet among them, in a crossfire of desires, dreams, passions, hidden longings and unconcealed demands, it seemed that she felt comfortable at the fo-cus of emotions, where the envy, wonder, or annoyed impotence of the women's glances, alongside those of the men, still shot out ferocious sparks around her. Her steps carried her along with unconscious assurance, as if she were unaware where she was going; her fixed smile was addressed to everyone and no one, if not to herself alone; and only now did she disclose to them her right hand, raising an ice-cream cone adorned with fruit and decked out like a masterly flower-cup, in a crazy impetus of alms-giving, as it were—yet even that may be simply in order that no driblet from it should fall onto her dress.

She was stunning, the way she was approaching, the blood-stained sun behind her with an explosive flare of light in the upper-story window of a building, as if Babylon were burning. She was somewhat at variance with the type that was usual hereabouts: slim, willowy, clear-browed, dark-eyed, her nose nobly chiseled. Her colorful, distinctively cut summer dress billowed to the ground but left her shoulders and lower arms free; on her neck, wrist, and fingers there were rings, strings, hoops, bracelets; on her head, a sort of tiny hat, or maybe rather a headdress, of the kind those interested might last have encountered in the photographs of an Italian (Venetian perhaps?) fashion magazine.

She was stunning, to be sure, and yet there was something lacerated about the woman. Some desperation of effort in her glamour; something of the sleepwalker in her assurance; some hidden feature about her beauty that verged on the ugly, threatening to break loose at any moment and gain an upper hand over the face in an unexpected twitch.

So what was the woman? A witch? A corrupting spirit? Where had he seen her face before? In close-up on a film screen, in a devotional picture, or on the front page of some pornographic magazine? Was she indeed corrupting or, on the contrary, herself corrupted? Who would unravel this woman's secret? Here she was and yet was not present; she seemed to be offering herself and yet was ineffable, like that frozen confection in her hand, which liquefies to sugary water if a living mouth touches it. Everything about her was fake; her fakery alone was genuine. Yes, everything was clear, the connections had revealed themselves to the beholder: they were corrupting him so as to be able to declare him corrupted; corrupting him so he should be able to corrupt them. This minute during which she passed through the reverential crowd, mesmerized by its self-flagellating passion, was becoming legendary; this deceptive triumph, a blunder. Myths were being woven about her, and she was falling prey to those myths. She believed herself to be a conqueror, whereas she was but a credulous victim; or a destiny, whereas she was merely a spoil, flirting with freedom yet sleeping with tyranny.

It was done. She had vanished like an apparition, and in her wake the passions sprang up again, wilder than ever. Bags, sticks, umbrellas dashed against each other, loathing flickered on the faces of scything victors and victims who were falling into the dust; persecution, rancor, harassment in all directions, as if all that was shrilling in their ears, whipping their blind anger into a frenzy, was the incessant panting of monsters galloping over their heads. There a man was forcing a way across the road, running to reach the bus. He missed it, his calculations thwarted by a change in the traffic light: four cars were rushing in his direction along the

four-lane highway, overlapping each other in a diago-
nal sprint. Out of one of them—decrepit, its bodywork
a shabby wreck, like a skeleton—poked the wizened
face of a bearded old man, horror in his unvaryingly
dilated pupils, his mouth twisted in an idiotic grin; out
of the second, a male head with a Gorgon coiffure, the
mercilessness of a speed merchant and the pain of in-
exorability on his smooth-shaven face; out of the third,
merely an upraised forearm from the elbow up, only a
sword missing from the threateningly balled fist; from
the fourth, another bearded figure, a curious badge on
the thrusting nose of his car to reflect the cruel splendor
of the brilliant sky: an arrow about to be loosed from
the taut string of a bow. The quarry turned back with a
done-for movement, left hand raised—in protest? Im-
ploringly?—toward them; then he raced on, back and
sideways on to these Furies, until they were all covered up by the monstrous body of a bus spewing out
black exhaust fumes . . . and over there? Had someone
fallen? Was that someone hastening to assist? Several
had flopped down, and out of the knot of people faces,
distorted with pain, noses and gaping mouths struggling for air, turned upward to where a vulture-nosed
aircraft that was preparing to land seemed almost to
alight on them with an earsplitting screech, shrieking
"Wheeeee!" And as if the high-pitched squeal down
there were being formed into a muffled cry, an answer
that intensified into a uniform wail: woe, O woe betide
those who dwell on earth . . .

These words suddenly confronted him, then they
disappeared again in such a way that he could not tell

off the top of his head whether he had read them or heard them. He had read them, of course, but right then it seemed as though he were hearing them as well. He turned to his wife, but she seemed to have noticed nothing; she was sitting calmly in her place amid the doomsday that was pulsing all around her. Her head was slightly leaning back, her eyes half-closed, and the westward-bound sun, which had already reached the terrace, was bathing her face in the softening light of the incipient twilight. It now struck the commissioner that he was seeing his wife's image in the intimation of another image. Never mind, that did not alter the truth of the present in the least; and that truth was perhaps nothing more, thought the commissioner, than that his wife did not see what he saw. There could be no doubt what she was thinking: her self-oblivious smile was, as it were, a confidential answer to the sun; on her face was the ruthless carefreeness of bathers and the spicy promise of tranquilly rocking seas—at which the commissioner was suddenly gripped by a fleeting bitterness, as though he were unable to stand the weight of the rebuttals bearing down on him. His grateful glance sought the stranger who had helped him to see, but he could no longer make him out, either where he had been before or in the crowd. Out there, beyond the railing, everything kept on going, blindly, unstoppably; everyone did their own thing, and only their own thing, putting up with and pursuing this mundane horror with the indifference of habit and the suicidal assiduity of self-delusion. Yes: his knowledge was futile, his truth was indivisible.

He made a sign that he would like to pay and, gently touching his wife's arm, reminded her that if they were going to take advantage of Hermann and his lift for the return journey, then it was time to make a move.

## ANNOYANCES. CONFRONTATIONS.
## UNMASKING. RECKONING

The next day's tour of inspection called for the commissioner to go to a more distant district, so he rose well beforehand—because his wife was still sleeping, he left a short message for her on a slip of paper placed so that she would spot it the instant she awoke—and ate a hearty breakfast in the hotel's dining room, and half an hour later he was already making his way to the railway station. He needed to get to a small town by the name of Z. Was that a town or a village? He was not more fully enlightened by anyone; even the railway station's staff had to resort to their map of the network in order to provide him with directions and a ticket. It was possible to get an express train to the regional railway hub, a leg that took fifty minutes, but from there he could only proceed by slow train. Waiting for the connection wasted forty minutes—annoying, that: he had to utilize every minute of this last day that was being devoted to his duty before he went to the seaside with his wife the next day; and even more annoying that, even after the more-than-generous waiting time had elapsed, he scanned the designated platform in vain, because there was still no sign of a train.

After ten minutes of silent fuming, he finally intercepted one of the station staff and learned that the train was late. The only response to his irritated reprimands was a lazy shrug: it was an everyday occurrence; the train came from far away and it had a long way to go, so he could count himself lucky if the delay was not more than forty-five minutes, which is what he certainly had to reckon on as things stood at that moment.

In the end, the train was a full hour late, and on its continued journey it not only did not seek to reduce, but perceptibly rather increased, the delay—for instance, by dawdling for twelve and a half minutes, waiting for who knows what, at some wretched village stop. When he finally thought he was at his destination, and he stepped out of the station at Z.—which in any case struck him as suspicious—into the free air, the commissioner looked around in disagreeable surprise. Where was the dusty square with its wilted, stunted trees? Where the open highway that he still visualized, inviting one to pilgrimages on foot beneath this harsh sky, shimmering with otherwise appropriate mercilessness? Instead, what he saw was a rurally built-up, crookedly winding street, and all the views that opened up from there led merely into further similar streets.

He turned back to the station to demand an explanation, but at the inquiries counter they understood only with great difficulty that he was looking for a factory: there had to be one, he explained. Behind the counter window was seated an obviously naïve, unsuspecting young woman, apple-cheeked and with ash-blond hair under her railway cap. Did she at last understand? Or was his venture doomed to end there, between these rosy lips and pearly-white teeth (shoddily filled and replaced with gold in places though they were), which, with the patient smile of a mother speaking baby talk to her infant, kept spouting the same word: "Hewt-ee-rah-vay-er-ke, Hutyra Werke?" "Bay-err-ah-bay-ah-gay, Brabag," the commissioner replied. "Hewt-ee-rah-vay-er-ke," he heard over and over again.

Finally, in a flash of understanding that he had already given up as forlorn, it turned out, all at once, that they had both been talking about the same thing in respect of the signified object; it was just their respective conceptions of it that differed, which is when he learned that he was in for a further spell of rail travel. The girl stuck her arm out of the window's lower aperture to point urgently at a scruffy branch-line train that was just starting to pull out from the outer platform, and onto the steps of the last carriage of this, after a breathless dash, he just managed to swing himself.

He lurched along for a further twenty-seven minutes. Was this the final stop at which they had arrived at long last, or the end of the world? The track broke off amid bare meadows and parched fields; the two iron discs of the lonely buffers at its end seemed incandescent in the scorching sunshine. Up ahead, over there in the distance, the shadows of ponderous billows of smoke sat heavily on the flat countryside. The passengers—a few people who looked like farmhands or workmen—suddenly vanished from around him, silently and all at once, as if they had been plucked up. All that was left were a rickety wooden shack and a plump female railway official with a little red flag in her hand.

"Is there a service back the other way?" the commissioner inquired to be sure. "There is," was the reply. "The local goes back in an hour and a half." That was not enough; he needed more time, the commissioner objected. The station forewoman seemed to ponder. "There is a factory here," she said eventually; he had heard about it, the commissioner said. "Well, at some point in the early afternoon a bus sets off from the main entrance," said the official.

"How come?" The commissioner was amazed. "You mean buses are running?"

"Why wouldn't they be running?" It was now the turn of the female railway official to wonder. The service was timed to reach the branch-line service in Z., and that took one back to the same railway junction, where one could change again for the express. The commissioner looked at his watch: instead of the full day that he had intended to give over entirely to his work, the pitiless system of times, surfaces and encounters was again conspiring to limit him to just a few hours, he concluded.

But was he at least where he needed to be? The commissioner looked around. No, this flat and empty landscape, virtually at the edge of the world, could hardly be called a landscape anymore. This boundlessly deep expanse, to which he had descended, under so many vicissitudes, from among the range of hills— that, like the bottom of a well, more to be divined than clearly picked out in the distance, left him in no doubt. These dreary fields and mean ploughlands that the almost gratingly bright sunshine was laying bare, down to their parched essence; the misshapen roots and bloated tubers of some species of beet or squash that were squatting on the lumpy clods of earth, like their ignominy as it were. This pipeline that came to an end here, the soil around it poisoned by the greasy, black discharge and decay of the end-products—they were all in place. Here was the highway, and over there, a bit farther off—shrouding in clouds of smoke, pinning to the sky between them, menacing smoke-stacks, ferocious cooling towers, and gaunt, poised-to-lunge cranes—was the reason and cause of all this: the great Baal, the beast. Yes, there, in all the profusion of its frothing and freezing, sniffing-in and spewing-out, blending and disaggregating, collecting and draining-off plant, was the monster, the insatiable Moloch: the factory.

No sense in dallying: he set off along the highway. He had no ready, worked-out plan; on this occasion he was leaving it all to the moment, to chance, to impulse, so to say. Was he not doing the right thing? the commissioner asked himself, suddenly pulling up after covering a short stretch. There was a fork in the road here, just as there was supposed to be. Poking up from the ground was an iron post bearing a blue direction sign, and on that the name of the place: an amazing concordance, or just carelessness? Not very likely. It was more that it verified his foresight: in this industrialized region everything was doled out with such tight fisted frugality that it was barely possible to alter it without upsetting this grim expedience; and no ambition to change it, no compulsion to adroitness, was worth the risk of overthrowing the diligent order. In that respect he could wish himself luck; his calculation had undoubtedly proved correct.

He continued on his way, maintaining a forced march, his gaze held increasingly on the goal. He had been approaching it for roughly ten minutes in this manner when, all at once, sounds caught his ears. The colossus had spoken, no doubt about it. Its voice had arrived from deep down, from the maw, so to say: three or four heavy gasps, like the panting of hellhounds. The commissioner was brought to a halt for a minute by consternation and this unhoped-for greeting: had it perchance recognized him? Was it warning him, or calling him? Well, he started off again. This time around, whatever else, the tables were turned, the monster had no power over him; on the contrary, now it would have to serve his needs.

But how was he to force it under his control? The commissioner was seized by an abrupt desire to act: this highway, this scenery, this powerless brute in front of him were indisputably his; all were just awaiting his arrival, prisoners of his will—to create or reject them, to abandon them to the formless misery of non-being, or to give them being from his own existence so that, redeeming them from their anonymous materiality, he might breathe life into them: it depended solely on his strength and capabilities. Over there was a gate, not the authorized one, but what of it! Maybe he had been wrong, after all, not to prepare the way for his arrival. See now! he would have been able to penetrate farther into this pestilential organism, uncover its voracious entrails, grub in its insides. The effort and the pain of the operation would, at an unexpected moment, add luster to the lucidity of consciousness that would shed the light of indisputable certainty on this pitiless encounter.

Yet maybe he could enter it as it was. The commissioner, stepping aside to let a car pass by, stood pensively by the roadside to weigh up the available options. Would he not be stopped right away at the gate, though? Probably he ought to apply for permission. Industry possessed autonomous jurisdiction within its own domain; he ought to reckon with difficulties, with having to get involved in negotiations, having to make himself understood to foreigners, having to identify himself. And whether he were to come up against good intentions or fussy obstructionism, would he not, in any event, have to deliver himself into the hands of others, get embroiled in a tangle of regulations, expectations, unpredictable escapades, goals and aspirations that were irrelevant to his work, to say nothing of the time that would be squandered on all of that?

There was no other option but to walk around the factory, along its outer perimeter. Around it? Well, that enterprise would certainly swallow up all of his time. Yet time—the commissioner looked at his watch—was something he was already starting to run short of. Still, it was unnecessary to go all the way around; not all the sides of the factory were equally significant; in the end, he could make do with this stretch here, as much of it as was offered along the highway.

To it, then! Time was passing; the commissioner got going. The factory was not surrounded by a fence but by a wall, behind which nothing was to be seen except the towers, stacks, and buildings that rose above it. Let that be the worst of it! Could he not see, even though they were unseen, all its nooks and crannies, its twists and turns, its rails, the signs for no-smoking areas, its cheerless exhortations, its scant concessions, the cabling buried in the ground, the pipes winding about in the air? And if nothing else, its odors gave it away: this foul stench was, in effect, the telltale stink of certain chemicals; this singular blend of the smells of tar and raw timber planking betokened cooling towers—were their inside ledges not assembled from these planks, hauled up on ropes into perilous, ever-narrower heights above the dizzying lure of liquid splashing, roaring, boiling down below? Futile for the factory to screen itself with walls; futile to withdraw to the depths of its entrenchments, its sulfur-breathed caldrons, its rumbling hell-pits—there was no secret it could keep hidden from its lord and master.

Nevertheless, something was undoubtedly having an interfering effect. The commissioner needed time before he could account for the precise nature and quality of this interference, to establish what was causing it: the buzzing that was filtering out from behind the wall; the audible activity of these things, objects, and the invisible beings moving them around, the noises. A humming of machines, a clattering of goods-wagon buffers, the rumble of bulk goods hurtling into them, shouts ringing out every now and then, a buzzing of wires, a roaring of furnaces heating faces that were bent towards them in the light of their flames; the hustle and bustle, comings and goings that turned buildings and laboratories into beehives, the ground's rumbling, the air's shivering. It was obvious, then, that people were at work inside there, that work was proceeding—as if he, the commissioner were not even there. He shook his head.

He marched for thirty-four minutes along the highway without, in the end, any result worth considering, leaving aside these few observations, useful as they undoubtedly were. The red sun glimmering indistinctly through the motionless fumes was high in the sky, the heat starting to become intolerable. The commissioner often had to mop his face; from time to time, he was racked and choked by fits of coughing. Snarling, squat goods lorries, splattered and corroded from the muck of their loads, roared by him: the factory's beasts of prey, each hauling a consignment to or away from there, with a bellowing scurry. Yes, they were going about their work in a free and easy manner, with a shameless unconcernedness, as if he were not even there.

This segment of his journey was slowly coming to an end. Over there the wall broke off and, turning a right angle, took a new direction: What could he still hope for from these few remaining steps? Reluctantly, the commissioner acknowledged that he had failed. Despite all this indisputable material evidence, he was getting nowhere with these objects. But why was that? he racked his brains. Now that everything was here that needed to be here; now that he would be able to read the crime itself from the scene; now that every detail perfectly matched and concurred, what was stopping him from unreservedly immersing himself in them? How was it possible that yesterday, when he had found nothing; that while he had grappled with those false localities and had been able to level against them merely the absence, the idea, of their true forms and actual beings, he had achieved more, practically speaking, than today, when he had found everything in its place? Was yesterday's defeat a victory, and today's victory perhaps going to be a defeat? He looked around at this world of objects. Again the same thing happened as before his brief triumph yesterday, in the city; he had a sense of his gaze slipping off things, vanishing and being refracted by them, of his strength failing on these surfaces. Truly, he was forced to admit, there was nothing that could be done with them. He would go on, and they would stay here; they would stay here forever, solidly and irredeemably; their forms would stay here, their substance and odor would stay here. They would remain here without his having been able to interrogate them; the objects would provide no account of anything.

So, that was how it was. Was that some new truth, though? Had he not been clear about that? Had he not recognized it precisely, just as, once a person is beyond a certain age and certain experiences, one recognizes every commonplace ad nauseam? Had he not taken it into account when he decided on his trip? Had he not come in order to wrestle with it and overcome this shallow and intolerable truth? . . . Or, if it hadn't been for that, then for what? Merely to convince himself of his own existence?

The commissioner stopped in astonishment. He had unexpectedly hit upon this truth here, beside the highway, like a wayfarer on fallen fruit; and as if its fermenting juice had gone to his head, he was overcome by a mild giddiness. Was that what he had been looking for? Had he wanted definite evidence of his questionable existence? Yes, and this fact was now staring with such stark clarity, like this spacious landscape and endless highway in the hard sunlight—this was what he had wanted: to make a splash with his presence, advertise his superiority, celebrate the triumph of his existence in front of these mute and powerless things. His groundless disappointment was fed merely by the fact that this festive invitation had received no response. These objects here were holding their peace;

like uncommunicative strangers, they were complete and sufficient unto themselves, they were not going to verify his existence. Let him find it in chance or seek it within himself, accept it or reject it—that was now, as ever, a matter of utter indifference to this pitiless landscape and to these obtusely different objects here. It was useless to wait for an answer from them: they were not denying him, but they were not letting him in either; they were simply different. He could never become one with them, and he could not read anything more out of them than this apartness: measured up against him they were foreign, and if he were to measure himself against them—he was superfluous.

He hesitantly set off again. He had nowhere to rush to. Could he still refer to his mission? Was his assignment still valid? Here, where the wall ended and the factory now flanked open fields instead of the highway, a yellow strip, some sort of dividing ridge, arose at its foot: Ah, yes! The sandy path. A bit narrow. It really ought to be broader, a good deal broader, but still that was it, there could be no doubt about it, the wayfarer concluded. A lad on a bicycle was approaching along it; by way of greeting he raised a finger to the brim of his cap.

"G'day," the lad said with a dumbfounded expression: he must have looked like a stranger.

"Have a good 'un," he replied, and anyway was he not that in truth—a stranger?

He looked irresolutely at the sandy strip, then shifted his glance again to the highway: over there, farther off, if he were to set out with the factory behind him, on the left-hand side of the road, he ought to come across a square piece of land—hacked out of the ploughed fields, perhaps still enclosed to the present day, who could know? He was seized by curiosity. As it happened, he would still have enough time, and after fifteen minutes of walking he came to a square piece of land ringed by timber planking.

A broad, wide-open gate. What was this? Some sort of farmyard? The hoofs of animals and wheels of carts and farm machinery had impressed their marks in the clayey ground. And there now, a barn, and over there, at the back, where—offering an unimpeded view of fields—instead of palings ran a boundary merely of logs and beams, a cattle pen; a bellowing plaint burst up from one or another of the tethered beasts, like a sad horn blaring in this immense landscape.

A person showed up: What on earth did he want? A middle-aged farmer-type. He might be a fine figure of a man were it not for all that surplus flesh on his neck and hips; that nondescript thinning hair might still have a recollection of cascading golden locks; that pair of rheumy eyes, of the sudden glint of a steel-gray glance. And here comes another too, with earth-colored face and pitchfork in hand.

"Are you looking for anyone, sir?" asked the first.

"Can we be of any help?" the one with the pitchfork joined in.

"They didn't always watch over cattle here," he said, or maybe asked. The men in any event turned more sullen.

"How should I know what they watched over here?" said the first. "Would you be able to tell the gentleman, perhaps?" He turned to the one with the pitchfork.

"Me?" the latter spluttered indignantly. "How would I know, if you don't know?"

"We're only employees around here," the first one explained.

"We watch over whatever they deliver to us," the one with the pitchfork said, and shrugged.

"We work for low wages and do what we're told," the first one added.

"We're honest folk!" the one with the pitchfork chipped in. He stepped a pace forward, and the first chap, close behind—almost shoulder to shoulder—did the same.

"In any case," he asked, "what exactly are you looking for, sir?"

What indeed? A silence fell. Three pairs of eyes stilly perused one another. He looked round. The yard was empty; apart from these two men, there was no one else around. He was still incriminating himself in their eyes. Who was to say what might happen to him here; they might throw him out, or hold him here—tie him up among the cattle while they sent for the police. Tie him up and then forget about him. He might be left here, his feet growing into the muddy ground and putting out roots, penetrating deeper down, ever deeper, until they hit skeletons in the depths of the ground, around which they would be able to entwine fraternally, until the repose of petrifaction settled on his face; and his vertebrae, stiffened to minerals, would hold him eternally facing these eternal clods, which gave the impression of shapeless dead bodies, as well as this range of blue hills, faintly perceptible over the way, at the rim of the skyline, and even static, eternally unattainable hope.

He shivered slightly.

"Nothing," he smiled. The hand fumbling in his pocket pulled out a pack of cigarettes, and he offered the closed box to the men, the first of whom eyed it uncertainly.

"American!" A smile slowly lit up the face. The man with the pitchfork's resistance seemed more solidly founded, and the light nudge that he received from his companion's elbow did not escape the wayfarer's attention:

"I don't smoke, myself, but my mate will take a drag later," he grinned and likewise reached for the box. Thanking them for the information they had given, the wayfarer took his leave.

"Goodbye!"

"God bless you!" he heard from behind as he turned out of the gate.

## AT THE STATION

He had lost a lot of time; now he had to hurry if he wished to reach the bus. He raced at breakneck speed along the highway—it was practically impossible for him to cast so much as a single glance at the factory— and he still had to turn left to get to the main entrance. What a scrum there was already around the gleaming vehicle! One of the shifts must have ended; it was only thanks to his discreet elbow-work, plus the discriminatory politeness of the locals toward someone who was obviously not a local, that he was able to find a place on the bus, but as for air, he hardly got any of that among the passengers as they were tossed this way and that. On top of which, as soon became clear, the bus was still headed for a distant objective, well past his destination, the station, but among all these strange villages, localities, and streets, he had no idea where to get off.

He therefore had to make inquiries, and there was no lack of willingness; a whole chorus of voices alerted him to the appropriate stop.

The winding street struck him as familiar, but then these blasted village streets were all the same. Left or right? Maybe this old lady, waddling laboriously toward him in a dark headscarf and men's shoes, could tell him.

Now then, left: that was the way she too was going, he should keep her company, the old lady offered.

"Foreign, are you?" she asked after a few steps.

"Yes," he answered.

"You came to have a look round our town, did you?" she inquired.

"Yes," he answered.

"A pretty town, Z." The old lady squinted up at him.

"Yes, pretty," he answered. "Though to tell the truth," he added, "I actually came to see the factory."

"Ah, the factory," the old lady enthused. "A pretty factory." She glanced up again.

"Yes, pretty," he conceded. Onto what, he wondered, was this old bawd's glance slithering so meaningfully? Not to follow its direction would be unforgivable, and what the stranger saw was several clipped hedges, an artificial hillock, and on that a wretched Japanese garden.

"Pretty park," he hastened to comment, a compliment that the old lady downed shamelessly—poor recompense for her trouble, for they had reached the goal.

What a crummy, deserted, godforsaken railway halt! Only now was that apparent. Several waiting people were already mooching about on the platform, locals perhaps, or from that area, their all-disparaging looks gawping open-mouthed at the stranger. The train was late, of course, though—so it was said—not very. If only one could snack on something in the meantime, but there was nothing. An invalid was selling newspapers, so he bought one. He sat down with it on a bench near the rails and leafed apathetically through it. But then, on one of the back pages, all of a sudden, his eye was caught by a well-hidden news item. At dawn that morning, in one of the rooms of the grand hotel in the middle of the regional cathedral town, he read, they had found a woman's body. The chambermaid had noticed that the room was fully lit all through the night, and even at daybreak, as shown by the light filtering through the crack under the door. There had been no response to knocks on the door, whereupon she had immediately informed the hotel management. The door had been forced open; the person who had taken the room—a lonely woman—was seen hanging from the light fitting there as they came in. Around the unfortunate woman's neck was a ligature contrived from her own mourning veil—the fateful veil that the staff claimed she had worn over her face at all times throughout her stay, never taking it off in front of anyone. Investigations were still in progress, but the circumstances left little doubt that it had been a case of suicide.

The stranger lowered the newspaper. He stole a glance down the length of the platform, then snapped confusedly to his senses—but how? Surely he couldn't be looking for his accusers?

He stood up, then sat back down on the bench. His hand rummaged in a pocket. He produced a notebook and ballpoint pen to go with it, and a minute later he caught himself immersed in a rough computation of expenditures on the sea voyage that would be starting the next day.

AFTERWORD BY TIM WILKINSON

"But, ere parting with the reader, let me say, that if this little narrative has sufficiently interested him, to awaken curiosity as to who [Bartleby] was, and what manner of life he led prior to the present narrator's making his acquaintance, I can only reply that such curiosity I fully share, but am wholly unable to gratify it."

That, as many readers will recognize, is taken from very nearly the end of one of Herman Melville's classic novellas. It is indeed a singularly happy coincidence that the only character to be given a name in *The Pathseeker* happens to be Hermann, because that immediately helps establish a link with the writer whose name has been taken by the publishing house that has brought out the present volume. The link is more than superficial, because just as the curiosity of readers about the background and motivations of the strange central figure of Melville's 1833 novella, *Bartleby the Scrivener*, or why his response to questions about these, or even to flat instructions to carry out any task that is not strictly a copying work, is an invariable "I would prefer not to," so too readers may find themselves mystified by Imre Kertész's *The Pathseeker*. What is it about? Who is the commissioner and what is he doing? Who is this ghostly veiled woman who briefly passes through the action? Where exactly is it all supposed to be taking place—which town or even country—and when?

Answers to these and other questions are to be found. It is just a matter of knowing where to look for them. But let me first note a deliberate link with the popular American author James Fenimore Cooper, a contemporary of Melville, whose *The Pathfinder*, the third in the sequence of Leather-Stocking Tales, lends its very title (though nothing else) to Kertész's work, if one bears in mind that the title by which it is familiar to Hungarian readers has here been back-translated literally as *The Pathseeker*, as the sense of the Hungarian word is much closer to a searching for, rather than the finding of, clues. It is perhaps not entirely irrelevant to note that a small passage from the Kertész novella was the inspired choice that the French label Naïve made to be included in a CD that they released of Górecki's *Symphony No. 3*, where the Kertész work was provisionally called *The Sleuth* (the excerpt used is from near the end of "Annoyances. Confrontations. Unmasking. Reckoning").

The most helpful thing that a reader needs to be aware of is that *The Pathseeker* first appeared in Hungary in 1977 (in a volume pairing it with the novella *Detective Story*), two years after the publication of Kertész's first novel, *Fatelessness*. That, as readers may know, is a first-person narrative of the adventures that befall a fourteen-year-old boy of Jewish background going by the name of György ("Gyuri") Köves—George ("Georgie") Stone, as it were—when he is carted off to concentration camps in Poland and eastern Germany in the summer of 1944. This deceptively nonchalant story had taken Kertész more than a dozen years to wrestle into a form that he was happy with, and he met with rejection from the first state publisher to which he submitted the manuscript. As he records in the notebook that he published in 1993 under the title *Galley-Boat Log*, the rejection letter didn't beat about the bush: "I am bringing up 'this subject,' so I am told, too late, it is no longer of topical interest. 'This subject' should have been dealt with much earlier, at least ten years ago, etc. Yet these days I have again had to realize that the Auschwitz myth is the only thing that truly interests me. In contemplating a new novel, I can only think about Auschwitz again. Whatever I think about, I always think about Auschwitz. Even if I may seem to be talking about something quite different, I am still talking about Auschwitz."

What also needs to be borne in mind, then, is that Hungary—like all the rest of Eastern Europe, including the state misleadingly designated the German Democratic Republic—was at the time, and right up to the end of 1989, "behind" the Iron Curtain (from the West's perspective, that is). Among the reflexes that most people in the Soviet bloc acquired was not to ask questions, or rather to do so in roundabout ways, with allusions, with metaphors, with nods and winks and shakes of the head, and certainly not to expect truthful answers. It's not that these reflexes were unknown in the West, of course, just that they were more habitual (and necessary) "over there."

The fact that most of the cast of characters in *The Pathseeker* are anonymous hardly matters, of course, especially if one can work out exactly what they are doing. Bus passengers, tourists, waiters, and railway staff are not problems either, but then "what did that gray uniform and faded necktie signify? A representative of the supervisory authority, an attendant, girl guide leader, a cemetery guard?" What has Hermann to do with anything? Or the veiled woman, come to that? What is the commissioner commissioned to do? Where does he come from, anyway? No, those questions are not going to get one very far.

Maybe it would help if one could pin down the localities more precisely. For a start, are these real places? The first clue is not offered until some way into the second section, when Hermann gives the commissioner and his wife a lift into the town (not identified) and they pass along a tree-lined road on which "the poet, so often damned and anathematized, . . . had picked fresh, juicy plums . . . , as he remarked in his essay about the Romantic school."

The one further clue that it is fair to offer English speakers is the name Heinrich Heine, since it is a name they rarely encounter, except perhaps as one of many poets whose works inspired Franz Schubert to his wonderful *Lieder* (in this case most of the lyrics of *Schwanengesang*, for instance). In 1836, Heine published a typically caustic but shrewd volume in which he assessed German literature and literary movements, from the preceding era (Goethe, Schiller, the Schlegels) to his own day, under the title *The Romantic School*. This contains such throwaway remarks as: "French madness is far from being as mad as German madness, for in the latter, as Polonius would say, there is method." More to the point, he notes that "An avenue of lovely trees, with plums growing on them, connects J. with W., these plums taste very good when you are thirsty from the summer heat." This does indeed seem to be where we need to be. The place in which "from over there people had given speeches, they had governed from there . . ." Indeed, where there is a "famous hotel that had gained its name from the rhinoceros or hippopotamus (the commissioner could clearly not have been paying sufficient attention at this point)—at any rate a pachyderm of some sort . . ." All very heavy hints, if you happen to know what the author is getting at. And if you are thinking of a town that was indelibly associated with Goethe's "day job" for the grand duchy ruled by Charles Augustus—indeed, was the capital of that state, both then and also later on, after the First World War, when it was merged, as the province of Thuringia, into the new German Republic, which all too soon elected a chancellor by the name of Adolf Hitler—then you are spot on! Now just think of a less salubrious place just outside that town—in fact, the site of a concentration camp in the war that Hitler provoked. . . .

A shortish bus journey away from that town is a hillside, on a crest of which is a fancy wrought-iron gate, and imbedded in its center were what looked to be merely curlicues. "'J . . . j–e . . . ,' [his wife] tried to spell it out. 'Jedem das Seine. To each his own,' the commissioner helped her out." On the next day, the commissioner has to take two trains to reach "a small town by the name of Z. Was that a town or a village? He was not more fully enlightened by anyone . . . " There is certainly a big factory in or near it, which leaves traces, both auditory ("all at once, sounds caught his ears. The colossus had spoken, no doubt about it. Its voice had arrived from deep down, from the maw, so to say: three or four heavy gasps, like the panting of hellhounds") and olfactory ("this singular blend of the smells of tar and raw timber planking betokened cooling towers"). Moreover, leading away from the factory's perimeter "a yellow strip, some sort of dividing ridge, arose at its foot: Ah yes! The sandy path. A bit narrow; it really ought to be broader, a good deal broader, but still that was it," which in turn ought to lead to "a square piece of land—hacked out of the ploughed fields, perhaps still enclosed to the present day, who could know?"

"Ah, Bartleby! Ah, humanity!"

TITLES IN THE COMPANION SERIES
**THE ART OF THE NOVELLA**

THE ART OF THE NOVELLA

THE CONTEMPORARY ART OF THE NOVELLA